Mary Anne Misses Logan

**Other books by
Ann M. Martin**

Ma and Pa Dracula
Yours Turly, Shirley
Ten Kids, No Pets
Slam Book
Just a Summer Romance
Missing Since Monday
With You and Without You
Me and Katie (the Pest)
Stage Fright
Inside Out
Bummer Summer

Mary Anne Misses Logan
Ann M. Martin

AN
APPLE
PAPERBACK

SCHOLASTIC INC.
New York Toronto London Auckland Sydney

Cover art by Hodges Soileau

ISBN 0-590-43569-8

12 11 10 9 8 7 6 5 4   4 5 6/9

Printed in the U.S.A.   40

First Scholastic printing, August 1991

For Joe, Monica, and "the boys"

CHAPTER 1

I missed Logan.

I had been missing him for some time. And the missing hurt. Logan and I used to be so close that we were almost part of each other. Sometimes I knew what he was thinking; we didn't even need to talk.

I am Mary Anne Spier, and Logan Bruno is my boyfriend. I mean, he used to be. But awhile ago I told him I needed some time away from him, and before I knew it, we had broken up. (Well, that's not *exactly* how it happened.)

It was a dreary Thursday afternoon, cool and drizzly. Rain had been falling since the night before, and the sky had been overcast for two days before that. So I was sitting by the window in our living room, looking out at the mist and brooding. I was brooding about two things — Logan, and this huge English assignment that had been given to all of us eighth-graders at Stoneybrook Middle School (or SMS) here in Stoneybrook, Connecticut.

I am a pretty good brooder.

Especially when I am alone.

And I was alone that afternoon. My dad and my stepmother were at work, and my stepsister was baby-sitting. My stepsister is Dawn Schafer, and she happens to be one of my two best friends. She's also an eighth-grader at SMS.

I was waiting around to baby-sit, too. Later that afternoon I would be picked up and driven to the Kormans' house, where I would sit with their three children — Bill, Melody, and Skylar — until about nine-thirty. My friends and I baby-sit a lot. In fact, we baby-sit so much that we've formed a business called the Baby-sitters Club (or the BSC). A bunch of my friends and I are the regular club members. Six of us live in my neighborhood, but our club president, Kristy Thomas, lives in a fancy area across town, where she moved when her mom got remarried. The Kormans live across the street and one house up from Kristy. I haven't baby-sat for them too often. Partly, this is because they are new here. (They moved into the house where a family named Delaney used to live.) Anyway, since Kristy lives so close by, she baby-sits for the Kormans more than the rest of us do.

It's funny, I thought. Sometimes I feel lonelier when I've gotten used to having a lot of people around than when I've been spending time by myself. I don't know why this is true, but it is, at least for me. See, for the longest time I lived with just my dad. My mother died when I was really little, and I don't remember her. After that it was Dad and me on our own. And I spent a lot of time alone. That was mostly because I didn't have any brothers or sisters, but also because my father was really strict with me. I think he wanted to prove to everyone that he could raise a daughter just fine, and be both a father and a mother to me. But he made up all these rules! He told me what to wear, how to fix my hair, and how to decorate my room. He wouldn't let me ride my bicycle downtown or talk on the phone after dinner unless I was talking about homework. And I had to go to bed unreasonably early. It was no wonder I hardly had any friends, except for Kristy Thomas. (We used to live next door to each other. That was before we both moved. Kristy is my other best friend.)

But things began to change, first slowly, then quite suddenly. The slow changes started when I was *finally* able to convince my father that I was a middle-schooler, not a baby, and that I was responsible, honest, and all those other good things. When Dad realized that, he loosened the reins. He let me wear my hair however I wanted instead of in two braids. He let me choose my own clothes. (Within reason. I'm not allowed to wear *really* cool things, such as cowboy boots, the way most of my friends are. And I'm *still* not allowed to get my ears pierced, although Dad lets me wear clip-ons.) Dad also lightened up on the telephone and bedtime rules.

Then came the sudden change. My dad met (actually, I guess he remet) his high school sweetheart, Dawn Schafer's mother. The Schafers had been living in California, but when they got divorced, Mrs. Schafer, Dawn, and Dawn's younger brother, Jeff, moved back here to Stoneybrook. And then Dad and Sharon (that's Mrs. Shafer) got together (okay, Dawn and I *got them* together), they dated for what seemed like ages, and finally they got married! That was the sudden change. After the wedding, Dad and I and my kitten, Tigger, moved into Dawn's house, because it's bigger. (In case you're interested, it's a colonial farm-house with a *real* secret passage that might be haunted.) So that's where I live with my new family. Oh, except for Jeff. Jeff never adjusted to life in Connecticut, so he moved back to California, and now he lives there with his dad.

Sometime during all these changes, I met

Logan, and we became friends and started going out together. This was odd for a couple of reasons. One, if Dad had been as strict as he used to be, I would never have been allowed to date Logan or anyone else. Two, I am the shyest of all my friends — and I was the first to start dating a boy steadily.

As I said before, Logan and I grew so close I felt as if we were almost a part of each other. We shared secrets, and we understood each other perfectly. At least, I thought we did. But I began to feel sort of smothered by Logan. Since he knew that I was shy and didn't necessarily speak up (even though I was *honest* with him), he began to take charge of things. He would expect me always to be free to go out with him, he'd choose the movie we were going to see, and sometimes he'd even order for me in restaurants — without asking what I wanted to eat. He wasn't letting me be me. So after a lot of thinking (and believe me, this took every ounce of courage I had), I finally told Logan I wanted to cool our relationship. I needed time to consider things. Only I guess I took too long, or maybe Logan took things the wrong way. At any rate, our relationship cooled off so much that it froze and snapped in two.

And so I missed Logan.

And I felt lonelier than I ever had when I

was an "alone" person and didn't know what I was missing. Now I had a family and lots of friends, but they weren't around that afternoon and I needed to talk to somebody. To Dawn or Dad or Kristy, or my other friends from the BSC: Stacey or Jessi or Claudia or Mallory.

Or to Logan.

I realized that he was the one I really wanted to talk to and be with. Dad and Sharon (my stepmother) give great parent advice, and Dawn and my friends are the best — they're people with whom I hope I'll be friends for the rest of my life. But Logan is a boy (he's also *Logan*), so my relationship with him is different from my relationship with my parents or my friends.

Aside from the special understanding we share, Logan provides romance. Only he could give me a hug and a kiss in just the right way and tell me that I would do fine on the English assignment.

I groaned.

The English assignment.

Thinking about what my teacher had told our class today was like remembering a bad dream.

"Right, Tigger?" I said. "It was a nightmare."

Tigger had jumped into my lap and was

purring furiously. *He* didn't have anything to worry about, except maybe whether some irresponsible person would close the door to the closet in which his litter box is kept.

"Oh, Tiggy, Tiggy, Tiggy," I whispered. I stroked his gray, stripy fur. I hoped he would settle down for a nap in my lap, which would be comforting, but instead, he took off on a wild tear around the living room. He raced over chairs and couches, allowed himself to be startled by a tiny piece of paper on the floor (he leaped into the air, all four feet leaving the ground, and his tail puffed into the shape of a bottle brush), and then he hurtled himself out of the room.

I sighed, thinking of the English assignment again. This is what our teacher had said: We were going to be randomly assigned to groups of about four people, and each group would then be given the name of an author to study. *That* didn't sound so bad, although I don't exactly love working in a group. I'd rather work alone, or at least with people I choose myself. The bad part was that this assignment was being given not just to our class, but to our entire *grade*. That meant you could be grouped with about a million different kids. Well, not really, but there are a few kids in my grade whom I don't like and definitely would not want to work with. (For instance,

Cokie Mason, who is my mortal enemy.) And there are even more kids I simply don't know. What if I ended up working with three people I didn't like or didn't know? I would be too shy to talk. They would think I was a real jerk. Not only that, but we were only going to be given a certain amount of school time in which to work. The rest of the work would have to be done after school and on weekends. I pictured myself over at the house of someone I didn't know, and shuddered.

I knew there was no way out of the assignment (except to fail English). I knew this because our teacher had said the assignment was designed to study an author in depth, *as well as* to strengthen social skills, such as cooperation. So I couldn't very well suggest I do an independent study. If I did, I'd be missing half the point of the project.

Oh, I wished I could talk to *some*body — Logan or one of my friends.

CHAPTER 2

If I had been able to reach anybody, I probably would have turned first to my stepsister, Dawn, then to Logan, then to Kristy, and then to Stacey McGill, Jessi Ramsey, Claudia Kishi, or Mallory Pike.

Dawn is a good person to talk to. She's understanding and she listens well, and she doesn't always tell you to do the things everyone else would do. This is because Dawn is an individual. (Everyone is an individual, but Dawn is a true *individual*.) She's not easily swayed by other people's opinions, or by what they do, how they dress, how they talk, etc. She dresses in her own way, which my friends and I call "California casual" — loose, comfortable clothes with a lot of style. Get this: Dawn has *two* holes pierced in each ear, so her jewelry can be on the wild side. Sometimes (since she *is* an individual) she'll wear one huge dangly earring in one ear, and two tiny nonmatching earrings in the other ear. In terms of clothes, Dawn could probably get away with wearing a burlap bag, because she's gorgeous. (Once, ages ago, she won a beautiful-baby contest!) Dawn has long, almost-down-to-her-waist hair, so blonde it's practically white, and sparkling blue eyes. She's thin and a health-food addict. She doesn't like to be within a mile of a piece of meat, she doesn't eat sugar, and she loves things like brown rice and tofu. Not my idea of a really swell meal.

Living under the same roof with Dawn has been both good and bad. The good part is, of course, gaining a stepsister who was already a close friend. There's nothing like knowing Dawn is in the next room when I wake up in the middle of the night suddenly panicked over a school project . . . or over Logan.

On the other hand, Dawn and her mom are pretty different from Dad and me. For one thing, my father and I like *normal* food — fruits and vegetables *plus* meat and cake and chocolate. (By the way, if Dawn tells me one more time that carob is just as good as chocolate, I will make her take a taste test.) Also, Sharon is a total scatterbrain, while Dad is a neat freak. Dawn and I fall somewhere in-between, and it's a little hard on us when, for instance, Dad wants to clean the house, Sharon says we can let it go for another month or so, and then they have an argument. There are smaller problems, too: Sharon is not a *huge* fan of cats (poor Tiggy), and Dawn likes to study with the radio or some music on, while I need absolute silence for studying.

However, I wouldn't trade these problems for my old life if you paid me a million dollars. I like my new family too much. Dawn and Sharon like it, too. When Jeff moved back to California, Dawn felt as if her family had been ripped in half, her father and brother on one side of the country, Dawn and her mother on the other side. Of course, Dad and I don't make up for Jeff and Mr. Schafer, but Dawn is happier with four people (plus Tiggy) in her house, instead of just two.

Now, if Logan and I were speaking to each other, and I had a problem and couldn't talk to Dawn, I might turn to him next. Logan is a newer friend than most of my others, but as I've said, we used to be awfully close. Logan knew what made me nervous or uncomfortable and why. And he didn't try to change me. If I felt self-conscious about dancing at a school hop, then Logan was content to hang around the punch bowl with me. He doesn't believe that the best way to conquer your fears is to meet them face-to-face. Maybe that works for some people, but not for Mary Anne Spier. And Logan understood. That meant a lot to me.

Logan is also very patient. I think this is because he has a younger sister and brother, Kerry and Hunter, whom he takes care of pretty often. Kerry is ten and Hunter is five. They're both really cute. Hunter has awful allergies, though, and his nose gets stuffed up, so he usually talks like this: "Hi, by dabe is Hudter Brudo." (That means, "Hi, my name is Hunter Bruno.")

The Brunos moved to Stoneybrook from Louisville, Kentucky, and they speak with this wonderful accent. I just love listening to Logan. He's not bad to look at, either. In fact, I think he looks just like Cam Geary, who is one of my favorite stars. He has long legs and blondish-brown hair. And his sense of humor is terrific. I miss his humor as much as anything else.

Kristy Thomas is my oldest friend and one of my best friends, but she is not necessarily the person I'd go to in a crisis. It isn't that Kristy's not understanding — she is — it's just that often her mouth gets in the way of her brain and sometimes (oh, all right, *really* often) she says things she doesn't mean to say. Kristy's been like a sister to me, though, and our families have gone through similar kinds of changes recently, so Kristy is pretty sympathetic where some subjects are concerned.

Kristy and I grew up next door to each other, right across the street from Claudia Kishi, in fact. Kristy has three brothers — two older ones, Sam and Charlie, who go to Stoneybrook High School; and a younger one, David Michael, who's in second grade at the elementary school. She has a mom and a dad, too, only she never sees her father. Mr. Thomas walked out on his family when Kristy was about six. Now he lives somewhere in California. After Mr. Thomas left, Kristy's mother had to scramble around to hold her family together, and she did really well. She got a job at a company in Stamford, and now she's a V.I.P. (Very Important Person), with an even bigger job there. Anyway, back when Kristy and I were just beginning seventh grade, Kristy's *mom* was just beginning to date this guy named Watson Brewer, who happened to be a millionaire and who also happened to be Kristy's future stepfather. Mrs. Thomas and Watson (I call him by his first name because that's how Kristy refers to him) got married during the summer after seventh grade. Suddenly Kristy found herself living a new life. Watson moved the Thomases out of their small house — in which

Sam and Charlie had shared a room, and David Michael's room was about the size of a closet — and across town to his mansion, which is so big that everyone who lives there has his or her own bedroom. (Well, except for Watson and Kristy's mother. They share a room, of course.) And you should hear who lives in the mansion now. Aside from Kristy and her family and Watson, there are Karen and Andrew Brewer, Emily Michelle, and Nannie. Karen and Andrew are Kristy's little stepsister and stepbrother, Watson's kids from his first marriage. Karen just turned seven, and Andrew is almost five. Even though they live with their mom and stepfather most of the time (not far away; just in another neighborhood in Stoneybrook), they spend every other weekend and two weeks during the summer at Watson's house. Kristy has grown really close to Karen and Andrew. She's also close to Emily Michelle who is . . . her adopted sister! Emily comes from Vietnam. She is about two-and-a-half and is adorable. Nannie, Kristy's grandmother (her mother's mother), moved in when Emily was adopted. She helps out around the house and watches Emily while the Brewers are at work and everyone else is at school. Nannie is a wonderful grandmother to all seven kids. (She's funny, too. Her old car is called the Pink Clinker!) Oh, also at Kristy's house live Shannon the puppy, Boo-Boo the cat, and two goldfish — Goldfishie and Crystal Light the Second.

Just a couple more things about Kristy, and then I'll tell you about Stacey and the others. Kristy and I look a lot alike. We are both short for our age (Kristy is shorter), and we both have brown eyes and brown hair. We used to dress the same way, too — like babies — but for different reasons. I dressed like a first-grader because my father was choosing my clothes for me. Kristy dressed like a first-grader because she couldn't care less about clothes. Now I've graduated to wearing whatever I think Dad will let me get away with, while Kristy has simply become the most casual dresser in existence. My friends and I think of her clothes as her "uniform." Tomboy Kristy almost always wears jeans, sneakers, a turtleneck shirt or a T-shirt, and sometimes this baseball cap and a sweat shirt. I think she's allergic to dresses.

Stacey couldn't be more different from Kristy if she tried. Stacey McGill is super sophisticated. She grew up in New York City, and her mom lets her do things like have her hair permed. Of course her ears are pierced. Stacey has blue eyes and shoulder-length fluffy blonde hair (not nearly as straight or as light as Dawn's) and she's thin. (Stacey is sick a lot. She has diabetes.)

Stacey is a math brain, but what she really knows about is style. You should *see* how she dresses. I've never met anyone quite like Stacey. She always knows what's the newest in fashion, and she puts together these chic outfits like paisley-print leggings; a huge, long shirt; short, black, lace-up boots; and a ton of silver jewelry. She might top off the look with a black fedora. Stacey is also allowed to wear makeup, plus she'll do wild things like paint a tiny heart on each of her fingernails.

Stacey may be cool, but she has not had an easy life. First of all, there's her diabetes. That's a disease in which her body doesn't process sugar properly. She has a severe form of the disease (she's called a brittle diabetic) and can get really sick if her blood-sugar level becomes too high or too low. To control things, she has to inject herself every day with something called insulin; test her blood several times each day; and stay on a strict, no junk-food diet. On top of this, her parents have gotten divorced, and Mr. McGill lives in New York City, while Mrs. McGill and Stacey live in Stoneybrook. (Stacey is an only child. I wish she would at least get a pet.) Stacey visits her father a lot, though. Sometimes she says she feels like a "commuter daughter."

Stacey's best friend is Claudia Kishi. In fact, Stacey is Claudia's first and only best friend. (Stacey has another best friend, who still lives in New York.) It's easy to see why Claud and Stacey are so close. They're very much alike. Claud is just as sophisticated as Stacey, but she's exotic-looking and, believe it or not, an even wilder dresser. Claudia is Japanese-American. Her hair is long and silky and black, and her dark eyes are almond-shaped. Her outfits are similar to Stacey's, but with weird additions, such as some of her jewelry. (By the way, she has two holes pierced in one ear and one hole in the other.) She likes accessories — T-shirt clips, slap-wrist bracelets, and for her hair, ties, beads, ribbons, combs, you name it.

Claudia *makes* some of her jewelry. She's a talented artist who's best at drawing and painting, although she also sculpts and makes collages. Her room is a wreck! Not only does she store art supplies everywhere, but she's addicted to junk food and to Nancy Drew — two things that her parents do *not* approve of, so she stashes mysteries, candy, and munchies any place where she thinks they'll be well-hidden. Talented as she is, Claud is no student, although she *could* be a good one. She's just not interested, unlike her older sister, Janine the Genius. Claud and Janine live with their parents, but no pets.

The final two members of the BSC are Jessi Ramsey and Mallory Pike. While the rest of us are thirteen, Jessi and Mal are eleven and in the sixth grade. They're best friends. And like Kristy and me or Claud and Stacey, they're very different in some ways, and very similar in others. They do not look a thing alike. Mal, who thinks she isn't pretty, is white, with red hair and freckles. And she wears glasses and braces. (At least the braces are the clear kind, so they don't show up much.) Jessi is black, with chocolaty skin, the long legs of a dancer, and no glasses or braces. Mal and Jessi come from pretty different families, too. Neither of them has divorced parents, but while Jessi lives with her mom; her dad; her aunt; her younger sister, Becca; and her baby brother, Squirt, Mal lives with her parents and her *seven* younger brothers and sisters. Three of them are identical triplets (boys). Also, Mal plans to write and illustrate children's books one day (she's always writing and drawing), while Jessi hopes to become a professional ballet dancer. She's well on her way. She's enrolled in a special school and has danced the lead in several productions. Mal and Jessi do share a love of reading, though, especially horse stories, and both think their parents treat them like babies. It's true that they're not allowed to baby-sit at night, nor to dress the way they'd *really* like, but at least their parents let them get their ears pierced. (Just one hole in each ear, of course.)

I stared out the window and sighed. With so many friends, how was it possible to feel down in the dumps? I wasn't sure. But I hoped that baby-sitting at the Kormans' would take my mind off things.

CHAPTER 3

"Suppertime!" I called.

"Is it hot dogs?" yelled Bill from the play-room upstairs.

"Yes," I replied. "How did you know?"

"Because that's what we always have when baby-sitters give us dinner." He paused. "Also, I can smell them."

I laughed. "Come on down, you two. Skylar and I are waiting."

It was six-thirty. I was at the Kormans' house, and I'd been busy fixing supper. Bill, who's nine, and Melody, who's seven, had been playing by themselves. Skylar, who's only a year and a half old, was sitting in her high chair. She had kept herself busy with Cheerios while I fixed supper. It's amazing how long a handful of Cheerios will entertain Skylar. She eats them one by one, seriously and fastidiously. Delicately she picks up one between her left thumb and forefinger. (I think maybe she's going to be left-handed.) Then she brings it slowly to her mouth and chews it for, like, ten minutes. After that, she starts in on the next one. All of this seems to take great concentration.

I was just setting the last plate of food on the kitchen table when Melody and Bill bounded in.

"I'm starving!" Melody announced.

"Me, too," said Bill. "I don't like our new school. It doesn't have good lunches. Not like our old school."

"And you know what?" said Melody, as she slid into her chair. (She lowered her voice to a whisper.) "My teacher is scary. I think she's really a warthog, but some monster changed her into a lady and then put a Meanness Spell on her."

The Kormans moved to Stoneybrook just a little while ago. They didn't live too far away before; just far enough so the kids had to change schools. They go to a private school, Stoneybrook Day School. Karen, Kristy's stepsister, and a lot of her friends go to a different private school, Stoneybrook Academy. Even so, Karen and Melody became good friends when the Kormans moved into the Delaney mansion, near Kristy. The BSC members used to sit for Amanda and Max Delaney, who were nice enough but spoiled and snobby, especially Amanda. The mansion is immense, and much fancier than Kristy's. In the backyard are a pool and a tennis court, and in the front hallway is a working fountain shaped like a fish. Well, it *could* be a working fountain, but it scares Skylar half to death, so the Kormans leave it turned off. It's funny. With the Delaneys gone, the house is as huge as ever now (of course), but it doesn't seem nearly as ostentatious (that's one of my spelling words; go look up the meaning) now that the Kormans live in it. The Kormans are much more down-to-earth, and I like Bill and Melody and Skylar a lot, even though I haven't sat for them too often.

"What's your teacher like, Bill?" I asked as I cut up half a hot dog for Skylar. I set her special plastic ABC plate on the tray of her high chair. (I handed her a fork, but I didn't really expect her to use it.)

"I like my teacher," said Bill. "He's funny. He knows good jokes."

At that moment we heard a *bang* and we all jumped, except for Skylar, who was trying to use her fork after all, and was completely focused on spearing a piece of hot dog with it.

Bill and Melody looked terrified, but I laughed. "That's the dryer, you guys," I said. "Your mom or dad must have been finishing up a load of clothes before they left."

"Are you *sure* that was the dryer?" asked Melody.

"I never heard it do that before," added Bill.

"Trust me. It's the dryer. I used to baby-sit when the Delaneys lived here. I know all about this house. Remember?"

"It's really scary, isn't it?" whispered Melody. She was eating her hot dog slowly, squeezing it out one end of the bun, leaving the bun whole. I wondered whether she was going to eat the bun separately or not at all.

"You think the house is scary?" I asked lightly. (I didn't want to make a big deal out of this, but I didn't want to let it go, either.)

Bill and Melody glanced at one another. Then they looked back at me. "Yes."

"Why?" I took a bite out of my hot dog, as if it deserved at least as much attention as a scary house.

"It's a *lot* bigger than our old house," said Bill.

"All sorts of closets and corners and dark places," said Melody. "Mommy said we could get a kitten," (for some reason, she whispered the word), "but Bill and I decided not to. It would probably get lost in this house and we'd never find it."

"You mean," I said in a spooky voice, "the Cat Monster would get it?"

I was sure Melody and Bill would laugh at

that. Instead, they both swiveled around to look at Skylar.

Skylar burst into tears. "No tat!" she cried. "No tat, no tat."

"What's the matter?" I asked, alarmed. I jumped up and ran to her.

"She's afraid of C-A-Ts," Melody informed me.

"Yeah," said Bill. "That's the other reason we don't want a you-know-what. Skylar would cry all the time."

"Why is she so afraid of, um, C-A-Ts?" I had lifted Skylar out of her high chair. She was alternately burying her face in my shoulder, and looking around the room for dreaded C-A-Ts, crying, "No tat!"

"We're not sure," replied Bill. "She just is. She likes to look at them if they're far away. But when they get near her, she cries."

"No tat!" whimpered Skylar.

"It's okay," I told her, rocking her gently. "There aren't any tats here."

Melody began to giggle.

"What?" I asked, smiling.

"The Tat Monster!" she said.

Melody and Bill became hysterical, and then very silly. While I calmed down Skylar and set her back in the high chair, Melody let out a shriek, pointed across the kitchen, and cried, "Look! The Oven Monster!"

24

Bill pointed out the window. "The Pool Monster!"

I laughed, too, but said, "Calm down, you guys." They were laughing in that way that sometimes leads to barfing at the table.

The kids paid attention. They calmed down. Bill cleaned his plate. So did Skylar. Melody finished her hot dog, but left the ketchupy bun behind. After a moment, she lifted it to her nose, began to giggle again, and exclaimed, "Watch out, everybody. I'm the Hot Dog Monster!"

"Okay, I think dinner is over," I announced.

Melody and Bill cleared the table, while I wiped off the high chair tray, then found a clean cloth and wiped off Skylar's face and hands.

"Do you two have any homework?" I asked Bill and Melody.

"A little," said Bill.

"No," said Melody.

So Melody helped me put Skylar to bed, while Bill settled himself at the desk in his room, his spelling book open in front of him.

"I don't know how Bill can do that," said Melody as I changed Skylar's diaper. Melody was poofing baby powder onto her hands.

"Do what?" I asked.

"Sit alone in his room."

"What do you think is going to happen to

him?'' I asked. Melody and Bill may have become silly earlier, but they were honestly uneasy in their new, big house.

Melody shrugged. She wouldn't look at me.

I set Skylar in her crib. Then I turned around and said, "Do you think Bill is going to be attacked by the . . . Tickle Monster?" I grabbed Melody and began to tickle her.

"No!" she cried, laughing. "Stop it, Mary Anne!"

I stopped. I drew a blanket over Skylar, who was already half asleep. Then I said to Melody, "Come on. Let's be Tiptoe Monsters and tiptoe to Bill's room."

"I heard that!" yelled Bill from down the hall.

We tiptoed to him anyway, but Bill was prepared. Just as we reached his doorway, he leaped into the hall and yelled, "BOO!"

"Aughh!" shrieked Melody.

"Shh," I said. "Let Skylar go to sleep."

"But he booed me!"

"Well, we were going to surprise *him*," I pointed out.

"This house is just too scary," said Melody, pouting.

"You know what?" said Bill. "Melody and I haven't even been in the attic alone yet. It's *huge* and mostly dark and — "

Creak.

"What was that?" cried Melody.

"It was the house settling," I replied.

"Oh, that's what Dad always says," Bill told me. "But this house is old. It's had plenty of time to settle."

"All right, then maybe it's getting creaky, like an old chair."

"Maybe," said Melody and Bill.

In an effort to calm them down, I read a chapter of *James and the Giant Peach* to the kids. Then I said, "Okay, bedtime."

Bill went to his room and Melody went to her room, and they changed into their pajamas. They met in the hall. "I claim the bathroom first!" cried Bill, and he raced into it and closed the door. Five minutes later he came out, looking worried. "I think something's wrong with the toilet," he said. "It's making weird noises. It's sort of growling."

"Maybe it's the Toilet Monster," said Melody, and she and Bill were reduced to giggles again.

Later, after the kids had gone to bed, I checked the toilet. It *did* sound as if it were growling. But it flushed okay and it wasn't overflowing or anything, so I decided nothing was seriously wrong. I'd just be sure to mention the problem to the Kormans when they came home.

I started downstairs to work on some math

problems. Before I had taken two steps I heard Melody call, "Mary Anne?"

"Yeah?" I tiptoed to her room. "Are you okay?"

"I can hear the toilet growling."

"I know. I'll remember to tell your parents about it."

"Okay. But do you think there really is a Toilet Monster?"

"Melody! You made him up!" I exclaimed.

"Maybe when I made him *up*, I made him *real*."

"I don't think so," I said. But Melody couldn't quite be convinced. I sat with her a long time before she fell asleep.

CHAPTER 4

I knew that I would tell the other members of the BSC about the Toilet Monster at our next club meeting. For one thing, it was funny. For another, if Melody seriously *was* afraid of a growling monster in the toilet, then my friends should know about it. We always discuss things like that at our meetings.

The Baby-sitters Club began with Kristy. It was her idea, and she organized it and got it started. What an idea! But Kristy is famous for her ideas, so the BSC shouldn't have come as a surprise to anyone. (Although, personally, I think the club could go down in history as Kristy's greatest idea ever.)

Kristy's brainstorm came to her back at the beginning of seventh grade. That was before so many of the changes in our lives had taken place. Kristy and I still lived next door to each other and across the street from Claudia. Mrs. Thomas was just getting to know Watson

Brewer. Stacey had lived in Stoneybrook for only a couple of weeks (I think), and Dawn and Jessi hadn't even moved here yet. I had no idea that a stepsister was coming into my life, and Mal had no idea that a best friend would come into hers.

But I'm off the track. When we were twelve and Kristy and I thought our lives would go on, unchanged, forever (or at least until college), Kristy, Sam, and Charlie were responsible for taking care of David Michael after school — if they could. But the three of them are pretty busy people, and of course they weren't *always* able to watch their little brother until Mrs. Thomas came home from work. One time that happened unexpectedly, and Kristy's mom was in a pinch. She got on the phone, frantically trying to find a sitter for the following afternoon. Kristy was in the kitchen, eating pizza and watching her mother make call after call, when she got her great idea. Wouldn't it, she wondered, be helpful if her mom could make just one phone call and reach several sitters at once, instead of wasting so much time on the phone?

So Kristy thought up the Baby-sitters Club. She and some of her friends would get together several times a week. People who needed sitters could call during a meeting. They'd be sure to find *some*one who was free to sit. Kristy first asked Claud and me to start the club with her. The three of us had done quite a bit of sitting, and of course we all knew each other. Then we thought we ought to have more than three members, so Claud suggested that Stacey join. Even though Stacey was a newcomer, she and Claudia were already friendly. The four of us were the original BSC members.

From the start, Kristy ran both the club and our meetings in a very businesslike manner. Immediately, she decided that each of us should have a role in the club. So Kristy became president, Claud became vice-president, I became secretary, and Stacey became treasurer. (I'll explain what those titles mean in just a few minutes.) By the middle of the school year, business was so good that we needed another member. That's when Dawn joined. Then Stacey and her parents temporarily moved *back* to New York. Only we didn't know it was going to be temporary. We thought it was permanent. So we asked Mal and Jessi to join the club. Then Stacey's parents divorced and Stacey and her mom returned to Stoneybrook. Of course we let Stacey right back in the club, which is how we acquired seven members. (I think the club is as big as it's going to get.)

I mentioned before that each club member

31

holds an office. Here are our jobs and responsibilities. Kristy got to be president mostly because the club was her idea. We thought that was only fair. Plus, Kristy keeps coming up with other good ideas — for instance, ways to run the club in a businesslike manner. From the start, Kristy made us keep a club notebook, which is like a diary. If I hadn't been able to bring up the Toilet Monster at a meeting, it wouldn't have mattered because I could have written about him in the notebook. See, each of us is responsible for writing up every single sitting job we go on. Then we're supposed to read the notebook once a week to find out what happened on our friends' jobs. So everyone would read about the Toilet Monster sooner or later. Writing in the notebook is a pain — but reading how the other club members solved sitting problems can be very helpful.

Another idea of Kristy's was the Kid-Kit. We each have one now. A Kid-Kit is just a regular old box that we've decorated and then filled with our own games and toys and books, as well as a few new items that get used up, such as crayons, activity books, stickers, and art materials. Sometimes, as a treat, we bring the Kid-Kits along when we baby-sit. The kids love them. They always find somebody else's toys more interesting than their own. The important thing is that Kid-Kits keep our sitting charges entertained and happy. So when their parents come home, they find contented kids. And then they're more apt to call on the BSC the next time they need a sitter.

"It's good business," says Kristy.

Claudia is vice-president of the club because she has her own phone, *and* her own personal private phone number. We hold our meetings in her room. That way, when parents call, they don't get a busy signal because someone's brother or sister is hogging the phone. And *we* don't have to tie up anyone's phone for half an hour three times a week. Plus, Claud's hidden junk food is the source of snacks for meetings. (By the way, we call Claudia's room BSC headquarters.)

I am the club secretary. I don't mean to sound conceited, but I have a pretty big job. I have to keep the record book up-to-date and in order. . . . Oh, I guess I forgot to mention that *another* of Kristy's ideas was to keep a record book for the club. This is different from the notebook. The record book is more formal and official. It's full of information — our clients' names, addresses, phone numbers, names and ages of their children, the rates they pay, and so forth. *And* it's where I schedule every sitting job that's called in. The appointment pages are probably the most important pages in the book. In order to assign a sitter to a job, I have to know when everyone is busy — who's already sitting, Jessi's schedule of dance classes, Mal's orthodontist appointments, and so forth. I am very organized. And I have neat handwriting. (I think my handwriting is one reason I got the job in the first place.) Besides, no one else wanted the job.

Stacey is the treasurer of the club since she's so good at math. This is important because she has to keep track of our money — both the money we earn baby-sitting and the money in the treasury. Any money we earn sitting is ours to keep. But once a week (at each Monday meeting) we have to pay dues. Stacey collects the dues, puts it in a manila envelope, and doles it out (grudgingly) when we need it. We use the dues to pay part of Claud's phone bill; to pay Charlie, Kristy's oldest brother, to drive her to and from meetings now that she lives clear across town; and to buy new supplies, etc., for the Kid-Kits.

Stacey loves collecting dues, but she hates parting with it. When somebody says, "Hey, Stace, I need five dollars for art supplies," you should hear her huff and sigh.

Dawn Schafer, my stepsister, is the alternate officer of the club. She has to be familiar with everyone else's jobs so she can take over any position in case someone has to miss a meeting. For instance, when Stacey returned to New York for that short time, Dawn became treasurer. Boy, was Dawn glad when Stacey and her mom moved back to Stoneybrook. Math is not one of Dawn's strong points. Besides, she hated the ugly looks she'd get from the other members of the club whenever she had to collect dues.

Jessi Ramsey and Mallory Pike are what we call junior officers. This means that since they're eleven and their parents won't allow them to baby-sit at night unless they're taking care of their own brothers and sisters, they handle a lot of the after-school and weekend jobs. This is helpful to us older club members. It frees us to take on more evening jobs.

So. Those are the seven people who gather in BSC headquarters every Monday, Wednesday, and Friday afternoon from five-thirty until six. However, I haven't yet mentioned that our club has two other members (associate members) who do not come to meetings but who are reliable sitters we can call on just in *case* a job is offered that none of us is able to take. With our busy schedules, that does happen from time to time. And we don't like to let our clients down. So if none of *us* is available to sit then, we phone Kristy's friend Shannon Kilbourne to see if *she's* available, or we phone Logan. That's right. Our other associate member is none other than Logan Bruno.

Sigh.

"Excuse me. Pardon me, please. Pardon me." That was Kristy, trying to get a meeting going. But everyone was talking.

"Hey, Dawn? What's a henway?" asked Jessi innocently.

"A *hen*way?" Dawn repeated. "Gosh, I don't know."

"Oh," said Jessi, who loves to tell jokes, "about three pounds. Get it? What's a *hen weigh*? About *three pounds*?" She turned to Mallory. "What's the healthiest thing to feed your brothers?" she asked.

"What?" replied Mal suspiciously.

"Purina Boy Chow!"

Next to me, on Claud's bed, Stacey was leaning over and peering at Claudia, who was lost in thought — and frowning.

"Claud?" said Stacey. "Are you okay? You look like you're having a nightmare."

"At *this* hour?" replied Claud.

"Oh, okay. A daymare."

Everyone laughed.

Except Kristy.

"Can we *please* come to order?" she asked sternly. She was sitting stiffly in Claud's director's chair, wearing her presidential visor, a pencil stuck over one ear. She pointed to the digital clock, the official club timepiece. "It is *five thirty-two*," she said, as if the rest of us had committed a crime.

We quieted down, and the phone began ringing. For the next fifteen minutes, we answered the phone and lined up job calls. When there was a lull, I told my friends about the Korman kids.

"They have an awful lot of fears," I said. "I think it's the move. You know, a new school and a new, BIG house."

"Are you sure they're not kidding about the monsters?" asked Stacey.

"Sometimes they *are* kidding," I said. "But sometimes they're not. Or sometimes they just take a joke a little too far."

Ring, ring.

Jessi answered the phone. "Hello, Baby-sitters Club."

The caller was Mrs. Korman. She needed a sitter one evening the following week. I scheduled the job for Dawn.

"Well," said Dawn as I penciled her onto one of the appointment pages, "I guess I'll get to see the Kormans and their monsters for myself."

CHAPTER 5

I would like to know just who invented school. And who made up the rule that every kid has to go? Didn't it occur to that person that some people might not *like* school? Actually, I'll admit that I do like school. A lot. (Most of the time.) But there are days I wish it didn't exist. Like the day we were going to find out the groupings for the English project.

I was a nervous wreck.

Please, please, please, I thought. Let me be working with Dawn, Claudia, Stacey, and Kristy. Our teacher had said there would be a few five-person groups. But I knew I had about as much chance of being teamed up with my friends as I did of winning the lottery.

Wait a sec! My friends and I *did* win the lottery once. We won enough money to pay for a trip to California to visit Dawn's dad and brother!

I grew very excited. But then I chilled out.

What are the chances of *two* incredibly lucky things happening to the same person? Almost none. (I think that is sort of the opposite of what's meant by "lightning doesn't strike twice in the same place.")

It was early in the morning. Dawn and I had already arrived at school. I was standing in front of my locker, twisting the dial and worrying.

"What if I end up in a group with Cokie, the meanest person in the world; Alan Gray, dork of the universe — "

"You're torturing yourself, you know," said Dawn. "They aren't going to post the groups until this afternoon. Why worry now?"

"You're too practical," I said.

"But what's the point of worrying? It's not going to change anything. The teachers assign the groups. We have no control over that."

"You're much, *much* too practical."

Dawn smiled. "Maybe the project will be a good experience for you."

"Yes, Mother," I said.

At lunchtime, Dawn, Kristy, Stacey, Claud, and I claimed our usual table. (We don't eat lunch with Mal and Jessi since the sixth-graders have a different lunch period than the eighth-graders do.) We spread our lunches on the table. Some of us bring lunches, some of us buy the school lunch. Kristy always brings her own lunch — and then makes disgusting remarks about the hot meal.

"Look. Lookit that brown thing," she said, pointing to a blob on Claud's plate. "You know what that could be? It could be something that just, like, *fell into* the pot while the cooks were stirring . . . what is that stuff?"

"It's beef bur-gig-non," replied Claud.

"Bur-gig-non?!" exclaimed Dawn, laughing. "That's *bourguignon*. You pronounce it the French way."

"How would you know?" said Claud. "You don't eat meat."

"That brown thing," Kristy interrupted, "could be — "

But *I* interrupted *her*. "Sonya Hardy," I said.

"Huh?" said Kristy.

"Sonya Hardy," I repeated.

Dawn looked mildly disgusted. "Mary Anne is *still* thinking of all the kids she could get teamed up with for the English project."

"Like Alan Gray. Gag, gag," said Kristy, pointing down her throat.

"She already thought of him," Dawn told her.

"You know what *I've* been wondering?" Stacey spoke up. "I've been wondering who I'll get to study. Wouldn't it be great to be assigned Lois Lowry or Madeleine L'Engle or Paul Zindel?"

"Or Megan Rinehart or Paula Danziger?" I said, feeling excited despite myself. "If I got to study Paula Danziger I would just *die*. Of happiness, I mean. Or Judy Blume or — or Robert Cormier!"

"How about Danielle Steele or Stephen King?" suggested Claud.

"I don't think we get to study adult authors," I told her. "I think we're studying people who write *young* adult books."

Kristy suddenly began laughing. She laughed so hard her face turned red, she began to cough, and her eyes watered. I wondered if she was choking.

"Who knows the Heimlich maneuver?" I cried.

But Kristy, still laughing and coughing, waved her hands at me. Finally she managed to croak, "I'm okay. I just thought of something."

"For heavens sake, *what?*" demanded Dawn.

"Alan Gray — " Kristy began.

"*Kristy*," said Stacey, all exasperated, "we've already thought of Alan. *You* thought of him. Remember? Gag, gag?"

"I know, I know," replied Kristy. "Just listen. I was thinking of Alan Gray studying Judy Blume. Can you imagine him reading *Are You There, God? It's Me, Margaret*, especially with a girl in his group? I mean, there's *bra* stuff in that book.''

(I should point out here that Kristy does not yet wear a bra.)

We began to giggle.

"How about Alan studying Megan Rinehart?'' I said. (More giggling.)

"Or that person who wrote *Little Women*?'' suggested Claudia.

"Louisa May Alcott?'' said Dawn. "But she's been dead for decades. We're going to be studying *live* authors.''

"Oh,'' said Claud, her face turning red.

"Never mind,'' said Stacey. "Anyway, this could be fun, you guys.'' Stacey looked right at me. "Stop thinking about who you might have to work with, and think about who you might get to study.''

I did. I spent the afternoon dreaming of all the great authors I'd like to know more about. I'm a big reader. There was a good chance that I'd be assigned to an author whose books I'd already read. By the last period of the day, I was terribly excited. In just a few moments, our big project would be underway.

As if someone were reading my mind, an

announcement came over the speaker system just then. "Attention, all eighth-graders. Attention, all eighth-graders. Your author-study project begins today. The lists of groups, and the authors to be studied, have been posted outside the office on the first floor. Please check the lists on your way home today. Thank you."

My heart was pounding. Now I was just waiting for —

BR-R-R-RING!

The final bell.

In a flurry of activity, my classmates and I gathered up our books and flew out of the room. Most kids were heading for their lockers. But I ran straight downstairs to the office. A few other kids had done the same thing. I was glad I'd arrived early. Already, it was difficult to see the wall.

It took me a minute or two to figure out how to find my group. The number 42 was printed next to my name on the eighth-grade class list.

"Forty-two," I murmured.

I stepped over to another list and peered at it until I found 42.

There it is, I thought. The people in group 42 study . . . Megan Rinehart!

I was ecstatic. This *must* be a sign of good luck. I adore Megan Rinehart's books. Imagine being assigned to study them. And her. It would be more like fun than work.

I glanced under Megan Rinehart's name to find out who was in my group.

And my stomach flip-flopped. I absolutely could not believe what I saw.

I would be studying Megan Rinehart with Miranda Shillaber, Pete Black (*they* were okay) . . . and Logan.

Logan Bruno.

In all of my fantasies, Logan had not occurred to me. How could we possibly work together? We weren't even speaking. Being in the same *school* with him was uncomfortable. How could we work together in a teeny, tiny group? There must be some way out of this, I thought, as I walked slowly to my locker. I just wasn't sure what it was. I knew I had to *do* the project. And I knew we students weren't supposed to switch out of our groups. So . . . ?

By the time I had reached my locker, my eyes were brimming with tears.

By the time Dawn met me there, I was crying. Actually *crying*, right there in school. (Well, I *do* cry pretty easily.)

"Mary Anne!" Dawn exclaimed. "What's the matter? What happened?"

I slammed my locker shut. "I've already

been downstairs," I said, hiccuping. "I looked at the lists outside the office."

"Oh," said Dawn sympathetically. "Who do you have to study?"

"Megan Rinehart," I whispered.

"But she's one of your favorites!"

"I know. Guess who's in my group?"

Dawn paused. She looked as if she were trying not to laugh. "Alan?" she said. And then she couldn't hide a small giggle.

I shook my head. "Logan."

Dawn's smile faded. "Oh, Mary Anne."

(Of course I began to cry again.) "I don't know what to do," I said, sobbing.

Dawn put her arm across my shoulders. "You'll manage," she said.

Wrong, I thought.

CHAPTER 6

Tuesday

Tonight I baby-sat for— Wait, here's a clue: I had to go on a monster hunt with the children before they would go to bed. If you guessed the Kormans, you're right. Mary Anne, why did you start that monster stuff with them? I think they're obsessed by it. (Is that the right word?) I can't tell if they're actually scared, or if they're just fooling around. Maybe it's a combination, like you said, Mary Anne. Anyway, beware of the Toilet Monster, you guys. Otherwise, this is going to get out of hand. And Mary Anne, don't you dare suggest to any other children that a monster lives in their toilet!

" 'Bye, Mom! 'Bye, Dad!"

"Good-bye, Mommy! Good-bye, Daddy!"

"Wahhh!"

Mr. and Mrs. Korman were leaving their house. Dawn was in charge of Bill, Melody, and Skylar. (The crier was Skylar. "Don't worry," Mr. Korman had said. "She never cries long.")

Dawn hoped that was true. Just then, Skylar looked pretty miserable. Tears rolled down her cheeks, and she stretched both arms toward the front door, which was now closed. She leaned over so far that she lost her balance and Dawn had to act quickly to keep her from falling.

It was a little after seven o'clock on Tuesday evening. Dawn was taking care of the Korman kids until about ten, while their parents went to a meeting at Bill and Melody's new school.

Melody gazed at Skylar. "I know how to make her stop crying," she said to Dawn. "Watch this." Melody held up her hands like claws. "Skylar," she whispered. "Here comes the Tickle Monster!" Melody began to tickle her little sister.

Since Skylar's cries turned to laughter, Dawn didn't give a second thought to the monster reference. A few moments later, she was upstairs with the children, getting Skylar ready for bed.

"Do you guys have any homework?" Dawn asked Bill and Melody. They were hanging around the nursery, using Skylar's diapers as headdresses.

"No!" sang Melody.

"Did mine!" sang Bill.

"Okay. Why don't you find a book or a game, and I'll come play with you as soon as Skylar's asleep," said Dawn.

Bill and Melody left the nursery. They were both wearing diaper hats.

Dawn dressed Skylar in a pair of pink pajamas with feet.

"You look like an elf," said Dawn, eyeing Skylar's round tummy and bulging diaper. "Ready for bed? Come on, kitten."

"No tat!" shrieked Skylar. But at least she didn't cry.

Dawn settled her in her crib, wound up her musical cow, patted her back, turned off the light, and tiptoed out of the room, leaving the door open a crack. She nearly ran into Bill and Melody, who were flying down the hall, diaper hats flapping.

"Monster alert!" shouted Bill.

"*Shh*," replied Dawn. "Skylar's almost asleep. I thought you guys were going to find something for us to do."

"We were," said Melody, her eyes wide. "But we almost got attacked by the Closet Monster. I was trying to get Parcheesi off the shelf, and the Closet Monster pulled it away from me."

"Melody." Dawn steered the children away from the nursery.

"Well, he did!" exclaimed Melody.

Dawn glanced at Bill. "I didn't see anything," he admitted, "but I heard monster sounds. Could you please check the closet?"

"Okay," agreed Dawn. "Which closet is it?" This would be easy, she was thinking. All she had to do was show the kids a monster-free closet.

"This one." Bill led Dawn to the playroom. He pointed to a door. "That's the game closet," he said.

"Maybe the monster isn't a Closet Monster. Maybe it's a Game Monster," suggested Dawn. But neither of the kids laughed.

Dawn sighed. She opened the closet door. *CRASH!*

The Parcheesi game fell to the floor, spilling its contents.

"Aughhh!" cried Bill. "The Closet Monster lives!"

Dawn disengaged Melody, who had wrapped herself around her leg. "A monster didn't do that," she said. "I think it was off-

49

balance from when Melody tried to pull it off the shelf. Look. Do you see any monsters in here?"

Bill and Melody peered timidly into the closet as Dawn turned on the light.

"No," they said after a moment.

Bill looked thoughtful. "Dawn, I think we better go on a monster hunt before bedtime," he said seriously.

"A monster hunt?"

"Yeah. You know. To look for the Closet Monster and the Game Monster and the Dark-Corner Monster and everything."

"I won't be able to sleep," added Melody, "until I know the monsters are gone."

"Well," said Dawn, "if we're going to go on a monster hunt, we better do it properly. First we need hats. Well, you guys already have hats, but I need one."

From a bin of dress-up clothes, Bill produced a baseball cap for Dawn.

"Next we need protective glasses," Dawn went on.

Melody found three pairs of children's sunglasses. (The ones she handed Dawn were decorated with Minnie Mouse figures.)

"Now," Dawn said, "we need a flashlight, of the antimonster variety."

"What kind is antimonster?" asked Bill.

"Any kind with red on it somewhere. Monsters do not like red."

"They don't?" said Melody.

"Nope," replied Dawn.

Bill made Dawn and Melody accompany him to the kitchen, where he searched through a drawer and unearthed a flashlight with a red switch. He handed it to Dawn. Then, armed with the flashlight, and wearing their hats and sunglasses, the three tiptoed from room to room on the second floor.

In each room, Dawn would shine the flashlight around and chant, "Monster, monster, wherever you are — GO AWAY!"

And Bill or Melody would add, "Yeah, go away, Mirror Monster," or, "Window Monster," or, "Closet Monster," depending on what room they were in.

Sometimes Melody would jump and scream, as if she had just seen a hand with long green fingers, or a set of gleaming fangs. Then she would say, "Okay, *that* monster is gone! Gone for good."

The last room to be exterminated was the bathroom that Melody and Bill share. Dawn aimed the beam of the flashlight into all the corners and behind the shower curtain. "Monster, monster, wherever you are — GO AWAY!"

"Yeah, go away, Toilet Monster!" exclaimed Bill.

Dawn and Bill waited for Melody to jump, scream, and say, "Okay, the Toilet Monster is gone! Gone for good." Instead, Melody looked as if she were listening for something. She cocked her head intently. Then she said softly, "I hear growling."

Dawn and Bill stood still and listened, too.

Sure enough, the toilet was growling. Apparently, it hadn't been repaired yet.

"Aughh!" screamed Melody.

"Aughh!" screamed Bill.

Dawn almost screamed, too, but she caught herself in time. And then she found herself running after the kids, who were fleeing the Toilet Monster.

Bill tore into his room and scooted under his bed. Melody tore into her room, scrambled into her bed, and pulled the covers over her head.

"Come on, you guys," said Dawn. She was standing in the hallway, trying to talk to both kids at once, even though she couldn't see either one of them. "You know there isn't really a Toilet Monster, don't you? You invented him. He's just a joke. He's silly and imaginary. So are all the other monsters."

"Then how come we went on a monster

hunt?" asked a voice from under a bed.

Dawn removed her baseball cap and the Minnie Mouse sunglasses. "We were *play*ing, okay?" she said. "It was just a game."

Dawn had to talk to the kids for about ten minutes before Melody would take the covers off her face and Bill would crawl out from under the bed. At last she convinced them that it was safe to turn out the lights.

"Good night," she said. She checked on Skylar, who was sprawled out in her crib, sleeping peacefully, unaware of Toilet Monsters. Dawn tiptoed downstairs.

Half an hour later, she tiptoed back upstairs. First she peeped into Skylar's room. Skylar was now scrunched into a corner of her crib, still sound asleep.

Then Dawn peeped into Melody's room. She couldn't see the bed very well, so she turned on the light in the hallway. Melody's bed was empty.

A chill ran through Dawn.

She raced into Bill's room — and stopped short. Melody and Bill were crowded into Bill's bed, Melody at the foot, Bill at the head. Dawn looked at them for a few moments, trying to figure out what to do, and also letting her heart calm down. She was about to ease Melody out from under the covers when she heard a door open and close, and then the sound of voices downstairs.

Mr. and Mrs. Korman had come home.

Dawn left Melody where she was and went downstairs to tell the Kormans about the Toilet Monster.

"What did they say?" I asked Dawn when she came home that night.

"Not much. First they laughed. Then they said something about the kids having incredible imaginations. After that, they paid me, and Mrs. Korman drove me home."

I nodded.

"Mary Anne? Is anything wrong?" asked my sister.

"I just can't stop thinking about the stupid English assignment. Tomorrow our groups meet for the first time."

"And you'll be with Logan."

"Right. How on earth could we have been assigned to the same group? To study Megan Rinehart, no less."

"What's wrong with Megan Rinehart?" asked Dawn.

"Nothing. That's the problem. Logan and I both like her books. I mean, I *love* them. And I think Logan's read almost all of them. So we'll both want to do a really good job on the project. Only — how can we, when we can hardly *look* at each other? It is going to be *so* embarrassing.''

Dawn sighed.

I sighed. Maybe the next day would never come.

CHAPTER 7

Well, of *course* the next day came. What had I expected?

I bit my nails through the morning, nervously trying to prepare myself for study hall. That was when our groups would meet. For the first time only, we would get together in the cafeteria, under the watchful eyes of our English teachers, who would make sure that each group could, in fact, work together without drawing blood or anything. After that, we would be on our own. We would have to meet after school.

How could the administration of SMS do this to me? They owed me something. A Ferrari, maybe. At the very least, a good grade. What if our group ended up at Logan's house — several times? I couldn't go there; not with all the memories his house held for me. And not with Kerry and Hunter spying on us and asking embarrassing questions like,

"Logan, is Mary Anne your girlfriend again?" It would be completely humiliating.

Maybe I should alter my appearance and run away under an assumed name.

But when study hall rolled around, I headed obediently for the cafeteria — which was a madhouse. I don't know how big *your* school cafeteria is, but ours is about the size of Canada. No kidding. It's a sea of tables and chairs and trash cans. With the entire eighth grade milling around in it, I felt like I was at a rock concert, only without a group to listen to. And without that feeling of excitement. And no fast food or — Okay, it was nothing at all like a rock concert. It was just a mess of noisy kids.

How were we supposed to form our groups? I wondered.

And just then I spotted Logan. He was running after Miranda Shillaber. So, feeling like a fool, *I* ran after *him*. I didn't call him, though. I just kept him in sight. When he caught up with Miranda, I stood behind the two of them. Miranda turned around and spotted me.

"Mary Anne! Hi!" she said. "Okay, now we just need to find Pete."

Logan turned around, too. "Hi," he said, sounding uncomfortable.

"Hi," I replied. And I was surprised to find that I felt . . . nervous, of course, but something else. I couldn't identify the feeling right away. I just stood there, looking at Logan, until finally I realized that I was glad to see him.

After all, I *had* been missing him lately.

But I didn't have any idea how he felt about me.

"There you are! Hey, you guys, I thought I'd never find you!" Pete Black joined us. "What're we supposed to do now?"

"Find a table and sit at it," replied Miranda. (She doesn't like Pete. In seventh grade he used to torment her. Once, he snapped the back of her bra, and the straps broke and the bra slid down around her waist. She had to go to the girls' room to remove it, and then she had to carry it around in her purse all day.)

"There's a table," said Logan. "We better claim it before someone else does."

So the four of us squeezed through the crowd of kids to a nearby table. We stood around it, deciding where to sit. Did I want to be across from Logan so I could see him, or next to him so we could sit closer together? I could tell Miranda wanted to be as far from Pete as possible. Preferably at another table. At last Pete sat down, Logan sat next to him, and Miranda sat next to Logan, so I wound up across from Logan. The first time I glanced up, he was looking right in my eyes! I looked back at him — but Logan shifted his gaze to the floor.

The cafeteria was becoming more organized and less noisy.

Pete, Miranda, Logan, and I sat like stones. We knew what we were supposed to do. Our English teachers had talked to us the day before. This was our one chance to work together during school hours when the teachers could walk around and help us.

But none of us said a word. So I was glad for a distraction. Even if the distraction was Cokie. She was standing by our table with her English teacher, and she was pretending to look serious and concerned.

"Is this the group studying Megan Rinehart?" asked Mr. Lehrer.

"Yes," replied Logan and Miranda.

Mr. Lehrer nodded. "Okay," he said. "Now, I know you were told that you could not switch out of the groups to which you were assigned, but I'd like to make an exception for Cokie here. She says Megan Rinehart is the one author who truly interests her. I'd like to give her the opportunity to study Ms. Rinehart's books."

I knew why Mr. Lehrer was making an exception for Cokie: because she's a terrible English student. Mr. Lehrer must have been astounded to think she was showing an interest in something.

I also knew that Cokie couldn't care less about Megan Rinehart or any other author. The person she cared about was . . . Logan.

What a snake.

We were going to be a wonderful group. Miranda couldn't stand Pete, I couldn't stand Cokie, and Logan and I weren't speaking.

Then Mr. Lehrer sprung his surprise. "Cokie was going to be a member of the group studying Natalie Babbitt," he went on. "Who would like to switch places with Cokie and study Ms. Babbitt's wonderful books?"

Miranda jumped up as if someone had stuck her with a pin. "I would!" she exclaimed, glaring at Pete.

I nearly gasped. Could this possibly be happening? Miranda was going to desert me — and leave me to deal with Cokie and Logan?

I thought of the Wicked Witch of the West in the movie *The Wizard of Oz*. "Oh, what a world, what a world," she had murmured as she died.

Those were her last words.

Now I understood what they meant.

Miranda walked off with Mr. Lehrer. Cokie, grinning, slid into the empty seat. She patted her hair. "So," she said brightly. "What did I miss?" She paused. "Why, Mary Anne!" she cried, as if I hadn't been sitting there all along. "What a pleasant surprise to find you in this group . . . and Logan!"

Logan smiled. "What are we waiting for?" he said. "Let's get to work."

"Oh, barf," said Pete.

Logan ignored him. "How many here have read Megan Rinehart's books?" he asked. Then he answered his own question. "I've read most of them. And I know Mary Anne has read all of them."

I dared to smile at Logan.

He flashed the briefest of smiles back at me.

And that was all it took. I knew then that I wanted Logan as a friend and as my boyfriend. How could I ever have said we needed time apart?

"I haven't read any of her books," spoke up Pete. "They're for girls."

"Pete!" exclaimed Logan. "I just got finished saying that *I* read them."

"You've read that one that has something about pink prom dresses in the title?"

"I haven't read *every one* of them."

"How many books did Marie Rinehard write, Logan?" Cokie asked. You'd have thought he was the only other person sitting at the table.

"Fourteen, I think. Right, Mary Anne? . . . And her name is *Megan* Rine*hart*."

I nodded. And suddenly I felt as tongue-tied and as awkward as the first time Logan ever spoke to me.

"Four*teen*?" repeated Pete. "You mean we have to read *fourteen* books for this project? How am I going to read fourteen books?"

"Oh, we don't each have to read all the books," said Cokie.

"I think we better," I managed to say.

"Of course you think so," said Cokie. She was answering my question but she was looking at Logan — as if she were hypnotizing him. (I half expected his eyes to turn into swirling red and white spirals, like in TV cartoons.) "You've already read the books."

"I plan to read them again," I said quietly.

"Wait a second," said Pete. "We don't even know what our project is going to be. I mean, we're supposed to study this author. Then we have to work on a project together. What's our project going to be?"

"It's going to be easy, I hope," Cokie replied lightly.

"Easy!" I exclaimed. "It's got to be good. Megan Rinehart is — "

"Megan Rinehart?" repeated Cokie. "I thought her name was Marie Rinehard."

"Cokie! Logan just — " I started to say.

"Logan, what's her name?" Cokie asked sweetly, interrupting me.

"It's Megan Rinehart — "

"You are so smart. Can you imagine what would have happened if we'd done a project and gotten the author's name wrong?" said Cokie. "Thanks, Logan. We would have looked like fools if it weren't for you."

"You're going to look like a fool anyway," muttered Pete. He was staring glumly at his hands, so he didn't see that Cokie was still hypnotizing Logan. (She could hold a person's gaze longer than anyone could.)

At the same time, Cokie edged her notebook across the table — until her fingers brushed against Logan's elbow ever so slightly.

Here's what we had accomplished by the end of study hall: We had decided to hold our next meeting at Cokie's house. (Well, *she* had decided, and Logan and Pete said that was fine, so I went along with everyone else.)

"Do you think that was a productive study hall?" Pete asked me as the bell rang.

I gave him a Look.

That night, I had trouble concentrating on my homework, even though the house was silent. Dad and Sharon were out, and Dawn was studying with her music off, for once. I kept gazing across my room at the row of books by Megan Rinehart that were lined up on a shelf.

I was glad when I heard Dawn call, "Hey, Mary Anne? Want to take a break?"

My sister and I wandered down to the kitchen. We were making tea when Dawn said, extremely casually, "You know what I heard Grace say today?"

"Grace? Grace Blume?" (Grace is Cokie's best friend.)

"Yeah. Her group was sitting at the table next to mine in study hall today." Dawn turned off the stove as the tea kettle began to sing. "Well, I heard Grace say that Cokie doesn't care about any author, not even Megan Rinehart."

"I know."

"You know? Oh." Dawn poured hot water into two teacups. "Then I guess you know about the Logan thing. No wonder you've been so quiet."

"I — "

"I can't believe," Dawn went on, "that Mr. Lehrer fell for Cokie's trick. He must be the only person in Stoneybrook who doesn't know . . . well, it's like what Grace said. Cokie just wants a shot at Logan now that he's available."

Available? Logan was available? Who had decided that? The dating god?

He was not available. He was mine. Well, he was once.

And I missed him and wanted him back.

CHAPTER 8

It was unbelievable. Unthinkable. Unreal.

I was on my way to Cokie's house.

You might be wondering why Cokie and I don't like each other. The truth of the matter is — Cokie has been interested in Logan ever since he moved to Stoneybrook, which is about how long Logan had been interested in *me*. And she once did a pretty mean thing as a way of trying to take Logan from me. This started a war — my friends against Cokie and Grace and their friends. The war began when Cokie tried to make me crazy by sending me frightening messages. She wanted me to look like a fool in front of Logan. Only I figured out what she was doing, and my friends and I got back at her — in a graveyard on Halloween night.

Of course, Cokie had to get back at *us*, so later she took things out on Kristy, since Kristy is the BSC president, and it was the members of the BSC who had scared the daylights out of Cokie — with Logan watching.

Now that Logan and I were no longer boyfriend and girlfriend (all of SMS was aware of that), Cokie had her eye on Logan again, *and* the three of us were working together on a group project. What a combination. I wondered if Cokie would have gone after Logan if he and I had been assigned to separate groups.

Oh, well. There was no point in thinking, "What if?" As my father would say, the cards have been dealt. Now we had to play out our hands.

Okay, so Cokie had decided our second group meeting would be held at her house (assuming the rest of us would go along with her idea).

Which we did.

I am such a wimp.

Now it was a Thursday afternoon — a beautiful, clear Thursday afternoon — and I was going to waste it in Cokie's kitchen. That doesn't sound right. What I mean is, I wanted to do a good job on our project. I just didn't want to do it at the Masons'.

I was riding my bike to Cokie's house, which was a good distance from mine. Not as far away as Kristy's house, but still pretty far.

This project was going to be torture. Pure torture. I wanted to ask to switch to a different

group so I wouldn't have to watch Cokie and
Logan together. On the other hand, I wanted
to keep Logan in sight. I liked having an excuse to be around him again. Besides, I wanted
to study Megan Rinehart.

When I reached Cokie's house, I chained
my bicycle to the Masons' mailbox. Then I
crossed their lawn to the front door.

Dum, da-dum, dum. Funeral-march time.

I rang the bell.

Please, I begged silently, let Cokie be *such*
a ditz that she forgot the meeting was being
held at her own house. Let her be out somewhere —

The door was flung open. There stood
Cokie, looking eager. But immediately, the
smile vanished from her face.

"Oh. It's you," she said. Then she added,
"Come on in," but she didn't open the screen
door. She turned and walked down the
hallway.

Now is your chance to leave, I told myself.
But I entered the house and followed Cokie
to the kitchen.

This was the first time I had been at Cokie's.
I'm not sure what I expected. Maybe rooms
that were as cold as Cokie herself. But the
Masons' house was the kind a person could
feel comfortable in. Cokie looked as if she
didn't belong there. The rooms were large and

cluttered, but not messy. The table in the kitchen was covered by a plastic cloth with pictures of fruits and vegetables all over it. The counters were crowded with magazines, boxes of food, jars of jelly. It was a farmhouse kitchen. And in it, Cokie looked like the answer to the question, "What doesn't belong here?"

Cokie pointed to one of the ladderback chairs at the table. "Have a seat," she said.

The doorbell rang then. I jumped about a foot (my heart jumped a mile) and Cokie made a dash for the door.

I listened carefully. When I heard Cokie say, "Oh. It's you," I knew that Pete had arrived. Like me, he followed Cokie into the kitchen, looking around curiously.

"Hi, Mary Anne," he said.

"Hi," I replied.

Pete looked sweaty. I figured he had ridden his bike to the Masons', too.

"Have a seat," Cokie said, pointing to a chair next to mine.

Pete sat. But, since he is not a subtle person, he started to ask, "Got anything to dr — ?"

The bell rang once more. Once more my heart leaped, and Cokie leaped out of the room. Once more I listened to her voice.

This time it said, "*Hi*, Logan! I'm so glad you're here." Then I heard the screen door open. Cokie must have held it for Logan, because *he* said, "Thanks."

A moment later, Cokie appeared in the kitchen, her arm linked through Logan's. "There you go. You take the seat next to Pete. What would you like to drink?"

"Oh, just water," replied Logan.

"I'll have a soda," said Pete, who had not been offered a thing.

Cokie looked pained. Then she turned to me. "Mary Anne?"

"Water, too, please." (I wanted whatever Logan was having.)

Cokie set four glasses on the table. She brought out a bottle of soda and a jug of water. She filled Logan's glass. ("Thank you," said Logan, and he grinned at Cokie.) She filled her own glass. Then she shoved the soda toward Pete, and the water toward me. "There you go," she said.

"Thanks *ever* so much," replied Pete.

I didn't say anything. I also did not pour the water into my glass. I was afraid my hand would shake.

Guess what. Logan must have realized that because *he* filled the glass for me.

I smiled gratefully at him.

Cokie frowned. Then she edged her chair so close to Logan's that she was practically sitting in his lap. "Well, let's get to work," she said. "What do we do first, Logan?"

"I've been thinking," he answered. "Okay, Megan Rinehart wrote fourteen books."

Pete groaned. "We know, we know."

"But," continued Logan as if he hadn't heard him, "who says our project has to cover everything she wrote?"

"Yeah!" I exclaimed. In my excitement over the Megan Rinehart project, I forgot to be shy. "We could choose three or four books that are representative — "

"Or maybe very different from each other," added Logan.

" — and just study those. Compare and contrast them." I knew I sounded like an English teacher, but I couldn't help it.

"I guess I could read four books," said Pete slowly.

"I read four books once," said Cokie, staring into space. "Four little books. *The Tale of Peter Rabbit, The Tale of Squirrel Nutkin, The Tale of Benjamin Bunny*, and *The Tale of Mrs. Tiggy-winkle*. I was ten years old. It only took me a week."

Was she kidding? That sounded like something Kristy would say in a totally serious voice — and wait for the rest of the BSC members to start laughing.

I glanced at Logan, but he didn't look at me.

"Well, anyway," he said, "we'll each need

to find a copy of the books we choose. But that shouldn't be too hard. Mary Anne already has most of the books, and then there are the collections in the school library and the public library."

"Which books should we choose?" I asked.

I think Cokie's brain resides on another planet, because in answer to my question she said, "Oh, why do we each have to have our own copies of the books? Why can't we share? We could read aloud to each other," she added, gazing at Logan.

"Yes, that's always been my dream," said Pete. "To read aloud to Logan."

Cokie, who had been leaning over so that her hair brushed against Logan's arm, straightened up. She glared across the table at Pete. "Pea brain," she said.

Logan, confused, cleared his throat. "I think," he said hoarsely, "that maybe we should choose one of Megan Rinehart's humorous books, one of her serious books, one of her mysteries, and one of her collections of short stories."

"Didn't she write any picture books?" whined Cokie.

"*Cokie*. We are studying books written for young adults," I informed her. "I don't think *Babar* counts."

"Megan Rinehart wrote *Babar*?" exclaimed Cokie.

Uh-oh. We were in deep trouble. If our project was going to be any good, it would be up to Logan and me to make it so.

Believe it or not, we accomplished something fairly important before we left Cokie's house that day. We decided on the four books we would study.

"Let's try to read them in two weeks," I said as we were getting up from the kitchen table.

"Okay," agreed Logan.

"Two weeks?!" exclaimed Pete.

"What are the titles of those books again?" asked Cokie.

I rolled my eyes.

Pete left the house first, as if he couldn't get out fast enough.

Good, I thought. I can walk out with Logan.

I hung around the front door. Logan and Cokie were still in the kitchen. Logan was repeating the titles of the books to Cokie. When he finished, I heard Cokie say in this syrupy sweet voice, "Logan? Would you like to go to a movie sometime?"

I did not wait to hear Logan's answer.

I pushed open the door and fled for my bicycle.

CHAPTER 9

Fridae

If I didnt know beter I wold think ther realy was a toilet monster. you shold have seen Bill and Melidy tonight. I guess I can understand why they thing theres a toilet monstir. The toilet does growel. But now the kids dont just try to keep the monstur away. They think they have to excape form him every time they fluch the toilet. At frist this was funny then it got sort of anoying. This is waht I mean:

The Toilet Monster had become a part of our lives. My friends and I talked about him at BSC meetings. (I *guess* the monster was a him. It could have been a her, though.)

Each time one of us sat at the Kormans', the Toilet Monster reared its head. And the story that Melody and Bill told about him kept growing.

Claud sat at the Kormans' on a Friday night not long after my horrible afternoon at Cokie's. I did not know then whether Logan had agreed to go out with Cokie. Our study group hadn't held another meeting, since we were supposed to be reading the books.

Anyway, Claudia arrived at the Kormans' in time to feed the kids and herself an early supper.

"Hot dogs?" Bill asked Claud as soon as his parents had left.

"Yeah. How did you know?"

"E.S.P.," answered Bill.

Claud shrugged. She turned back to the stove.

Bill and Melody were sitting on the floor with Skylar between them.

"Now, *this* is how you play Pat-a-Cake," Melody said patiently.

"Tat?" shrieked Skylar, looking around the room. "Where tat?"

"No tat," Bill told her. "Melody said *pat*, not *cat*. Pat."

"Where tat?" Skylar asked again, sounding pitiful.

"Hey, you want to get rid of tats forever?" Melody said to her sister. "I mean, only the tats that might be hiding in our house? I just have to do one thing. I just — "

Skylar did not understand, of course. And she wasn't paying attention. She had found a wooden spoon and a pot and was banging away happily.

(One thing my friends and I have learned is that you don't have to spend a ton of money on toys for babies. They are perfectly happy with a paper cup or an empty milk carton or a cardboard box. Also, a wooden spoon and a pot make a fine drum, if you can stand the noise.)

"Dinner's ready," Claud said a few minutes later.

"Oh, boy," said Bill. "Hot dogs and applesauce. Is it, like, a rule that baby-sitters can only fix hot dogs for dinner?"

"Yes," Claudia answered seriously. "It's Rule Number One Hundred and Sixteen in the Baby-sitters Handbook. It's in the section titled Hot Dog Laws."

Bill laughed, but Melody frowned and said, "Really?"

"No, you geek!" cried Bill.

"No, geek!" cried Skylar, which made everybody laugh.

"Let's see what else we can get her to say," suggested Bill, inspired. (As he talked, he pretty much inhaled his hot dog. Already, it was nearly gone.) "Skylar? Skylar, say *doggie. Doggie.*"

"Doddie," Skylar repeated obediently.

"Don't anybody ask her to say C-A-T," Claudia warned Bill and Melody.

"Oh, we won't," Melody assured Claud. "Skylar, say *come here.*"

"Tum ear."

Bill's eyes lit up. "Say *cowabunga, dude!*"

"Towabumpa, dude!" Skylar looked quite pleased with herself.

"Hey, Skylar, can you say *Toilet Monster?*" asked Melody in a teacher's voice.

"No," replied Skylar.

More laughter.

"Who here thinks it would be fun to play the Telephone Game with Skylar?" said Bill. (He had finished his dinner.)

"Not me," Melody answered. "Anyway, Telephone's funner with more people."

"Funner?!" repeated Bill. "Hey, everybody, Melody said *funner.*"

Melody blushed. "Is that a bad word?"

"No, stupid. It's — "

"I'm not stupid!" cried Melody.

"Okay, you two. Enough," said Claud.

The kids settled down. Bill and Melody carried their plates to the sink. Skylar, eating slowly and carefully (without the use of her fork), aimed a piece of hot dog toward her mouth, and missed. As the hot dog fell to the floor, Skylar peered over the edge of her high chair and shouted, "Towabumpa, dude!"

Melody and Bill nearly became hysterical, so Claudia sent them upstairs while she cleaned up the kitchen, and Skylar finished eating. She thought she heard the toilet flush several times, but she wasn't sure. It was hard to hear over the sounds of running water, clanking dishes, and Skylar's cries of "Towabumpa, dude!"

At last the kitchen was clean. Claudia removed Skylar from her high chair, wiped her face and hands, and started upstairs with her. On the way, she heard the toilet flush again. A horrible thought occurred to Claud. What if Bill and Melody were sick? What if the toilet-flushing meant they'd gotten the stomach flu or something?

Claudia raced the rest of the way up the stairs — and nearly ran into Melody, who was charging out of the bathroom, giggling.

"Whoa!" exclaimed Claudia. "What's going on? Why do I hear the toilet flushing?"

Bill emerged from his room, looking smug.

"Bill?" said Claud.

"You tell her," Bill said to Melody.

"Okay," she replied. "Um, Bill says that the Toilet Monster won't hurt you if you can run all the way into your bedroom and jump into bed before the toilet stops flushing." Melody paused. "Uh-oh," she said. "The toilet is finished and I'm not even in my room."

"The Toilet Monster is going to get you," said Bill. He curled his hands into claws. "*Grrr.* Hear me growling? I am an angry —"

"No monsters," said Skylar.

"That's right. There are no monsters," agreed Claudia.

Melody looked uncertain. "Bill?" she said. "If I ran into my room and got into bed now, would it be too late?"

"Much," was Bill's answer. "You're in for it now. You'll see. Tonight . . . while you're sleeping . . . into your room will creep . . . the Toilet Monster. *Grrr!*"

"Melody, Bill's just teasing," said Claud.

"I thought so," said Melody, who didn't look sure at all.

"Good. Now do you guys have any homework?"

"On the weekend?" replied Melody. "No way."

"Skylar does," said Bill. "She has to learn

to say all sorts of hard words like *Leonardo*
and *cafeteria* and — the longest word in the
world — *antidisestablishmentarianism.* Right,
Skylar?"

"You guys, I'm serious," said Claud. "Do
you have homework?"

"Hey, where's Skylar?" asked Bill, glancing
around the hallway.

Claudia panicked momentarily, looked behind her, saw that the baby gate at the top of
the stairs was closed, sighed with relief,
and —

"Aughhh!" screamed Melody and Bill.

The toilet flushed.

While the older kids dashed for their beds,
Claudia peeped into the bathroom. There was
Skylar. She was throwing handfuls of Kleenex
into the toilet. She was about to flush it again.
"Towabumpa!" she cried, as she reached for
the handle. She looked as though she were
concentrating hard.

Claudia made a grab for Skylar. "Hey,
kiddo," she said. "You're going to make the
toilet overflow, and then what will your
brother and sister think?"

The toilet stopped flushing, and Claud
heard cries of, "I made it!" from Bill and Melody's bedrooms.

"Safe again!" added Bill.

But Melody called, "Claudia? Is the Toilet

Monster flushing him*self* now? If he is, then Bill and I are always going to have to listen for the toilet and then race for our rooms. What if we're down*stairs* when the toilet flushes?"

"Melody," said Claudia, but she was interrupted.

"Towabumpa!" The toilet flushed again.

"Well, this time at least we're already in bed," said Melody nervously.

Claudia retrieved Skylar from the bathroom, set her in her crib, returned to the bathroom, put the Kleenex box out of reach, and went back to Skylar.

"Now, listen," she said, but not too sternly, "the toilet is not a toy. . . . Although come to think of it, *toilet* sounds like *toy*, so maybe you're confused. But anyway, Skylar, we do *not* flush things down the toilet, okay?" Claudia paused, wondering if she ought to clarify that statement by saying that it was okay to flush toilet paper. But she decided not to. She just said, "No flushing," and hoped she wasn't ruining anything Mr. and Mrs. Korman might teach Skylar when they toilet-trained her.

Claudia changed Skylar's diaper, put her in a pair of pajamas, sang "Old MacDonald Had a Farm" to her, then turned out the light and tiptoed into the hall. She stood still, listening.

Not a sound. She peeked into Bill's room. He was lying on his bed. She peeked into Melody's room. She was lying on her bed.

"Bill. Melody," said Claud.

"Yeah?" they replied.

"How *long* do you have to stay in bed after the toilet has stopped flushing?"

"I don't know," answered Melody.

"Good question," said Bill.

"Well, I think you'll be safe now. You can come out of your rooms. The toilet stopped flushing about fifteen minutes ago. Besides, you guys have to go to bed soon yourselves. You don't want to waste a perfectly good Friday evening, do you?"

"No," said the kids.

Claudia, Bill, and Melody played Parcheesi. They played a "tournament," which Bill won. When the tournament was over, it was bedtime.

"Which one of you guys is brave enough to use the bathroom first?" asked Claud.

"Me!" cried Melody.

She and Bill changed into their nightclothes, and then Melody ventured into the bathroom. A few minutes later, the toilet flushed, the bathroom door burst open, and Melody sprinted into the hallway, tripped, fell, stopped to rub her ankle, then limped to her bed. She was about to climb in when . . . the toilet stopped flushing.

"He's after me!" screamed Melody. She leaped into her bed and hid under the covers. "Check for monsters, Claudia!" she demanded.

Claudia made a point of looking everywhere (including in the toilet tank) and saying, "Nope. Not under the bed. . . . Nope. Not behind the curtains. . . . Nope. Not in the dresser drawers."

Finally Melody emerged from under the covers. "I guess I'm safe," she said.

Meanwhile, Bill found the courage to use the bathroom himself. Thankfully, *he* landed in his bed seconds before the toilet stopped flushing.

"Good night," Claudia said to Melody and Bill. She went downstairs, reluctantly opened her math book, and began her weekend homework.

Half an hour later, she checked on the kids. They were sound asleep — in their own beds. Good, thought Claudia. But not more than ten minutes later, she heard screaming from upstairs.

In a flash, Claud was kneeling by Melody's bed. "Did you have a bad dream?"' she whispered. "Are you all right?"

"The Toilet Monster got me," said Melody in a choked voice.

"But he didn't," Claud told her. "Not really. See? You're okay. You were dreaming."

"I heard noises," Melody insisted.

"Like flushing?"

"Yes."

"Melody, do you believe in witches?" Claud asked slowly.

"Witches? No!" Melody nearly giggled.

"Do you believe in Casper the Friendly Ghost?"

"*No!*"

"Then how about the Toilet Monster?"

"He's right in the bathroom . . . waiting for me."

Claudia shook her head.

CHAPTER 10

Of all the nerve.

Logan actually went out with Cokie. And not just once — several times. Several times that *I* knew of. Maybe they'd even been out more than several times.

How did I hear about their dates? Easy. Cokie has a mouth the size of the Grand Canyon. She just loved announcing to all of SMS that she was dating Logan Bruno. She especially enjoyed bringing up the subject at the next meeting of the Megan Rinehart study group.

The next meeting was the first one we held since the meeting at the Masons' house when Cokie let it be known that at the age of ten she had read four Beatrix Potter books in just a week. Fifteen days had gone by. Pete, Cokie, Logan, and I were supposed to have read (or reread) the four Megan Rinehart books we had chosen. I knew Logan had done this (or at least had almost done it) because I'd bumped into him in the school library one day, returning the mystery.

"Mary Anne! Hi!" he'd said.

"Hi." (Silence.) "Have you finished the reading?" I finally asked.

"Except for the collection of short stories. But that's at home and I'll get to it."

"Great!"

"Yeah. How about you?"

"I just had to reread the books. I finished last night."

(More silence.)

Logan nodded his head. "Well . . . see ya."

"See ya."

Now Pete, Cokie, and I were sitting around in Pete's basement rec room. We were waiting for Logan to arrive. While we waited, Cokie said, "I just saw the best film. It was a funny old movie called *Top Hat*. All this dancing was in it. . . . I saw it last night. With Logan." Cokie slid her gaze from Pete to me.

"What was it about?" asked Pete.

"Oh. . . . You know? I'm not sure. Logan and I weren't paying much attention. We were sharing this box of popcorn. And Logan kept saying he should go home so he could read the books, but I wouldn't let him."

"Speaking of our books," I interrupted Cokie, "did you guys read them?"

Pete smiled a genuine smile. "I actually did," he said. "All four of them. And you know what? I *liked* them. Especially the funny one."

"Oh, me, too," agreed Cokie quickly. "That funny one was so . . . *fun*ny."

"Wasn't it?" I said. "I could read *Louie Strikes Again* over and over."

"So could I." Cokie sighed, as if deeply satisfied.

But Pete gave us a funny look. "The book," he said, "is not called *Louie Strikes Again*. It's called — "

Cokie was saved by the doorbell. Logan had arrived.

All right. Now I knew that Cokie hadn't read Megan Rinehart's humorous book. She probably hadn't read the others, either.

Cokie bounded upstairs to greet Logan, even though she was in Pete's house.

I looked at Pete. He seemed totally confused. No wonder. For one thing, he'd gotten to his feet to answer the door, but Cokie had beaten him to it. For another, he was still pondering *Louie Strikes Again*.

"Mary Anne," he said, "what's with *Louie Strikes Again*? That isn't a Megan Rinehart book. I thought you knew all of her work."

"Don't worry," I said to Pete. "I know that isn't one of her books. I was just testing Cokie.

I bet she hasn't done any of the reading."

Pete frowned. Before he could say anything, though, Cokie returned with Logan. They had linked arms. And as they walked down the stairs, they bent their heads together while Cokie whispered something. Then they smiled.

Logan and Cokie plopped onto this old, scarred leather couch.

"Hi, Mary Anne. Hi, Pete," said Logan.

"Hi," we replied.

I wanted to cry, but of course, I didn't. I have cried at some embarrassing times, but even I could hold back the tears when I was faced with Logan and . . . Cokie. It was a pretty hard sight to take in, though. I remembered when *I* used to sit next to Logan, sometimes leaning against him or even resting my head on his shoulder. I also remembered all the times we'd gone to school dances — and not danced. Or when we had stayed home from parties because I was too shy to go. Logan would never have that problem with Cokie. She loved to dance and party and go out. No one could describe *her* as shy.

"My life," said Cokie out of the blue, "has just been a whirlwind lately. Logan and I have been so busy."

"I guess that's why you haven't been able to do the reading," Pete said.

Cokie went on talking as if Pete had not spoken. "Let's see. We went to a concert in Stamford one night."

(A concert? Logan and I had never gone to a concert. Well, there was this one we wanted to go to, but it was being held on a school night and I had to take a test the next day so I said I thought we better not go, and Logan said okay.)

"And," Cokie continued, "we've been to two — no, three — movies. Plus all those games at school. Boy, are our teams doing well."

Logan must have loved having a girlfriend who would go to games with him. I hardly ever wanted to. (But when did Logan have time to work? I wondered.)

Uh-oh. Had I just referred to Cokie as Logan's *girlfriend?* She couldn't really be. She and Logan were only good friends . . . right?

I had no idea. All I knew was that I ached for Logan. And that if Cokie kept talking about him, I might go crazy.

So when Cokie finally stopped talking, I asked, "Did anyone have trouble finding the Megan Rinehart books?"

"Nope," replied Pete. "I found 'em all."

Logan shook his head.

Cokie could not look at me. I bet she was thinking about her *Louie Strikes Again* mistake.

. . . And was she blushing just a little?

"So we've all done the reading?" I said.

"Yup," replied Pete.

Logan and Cokie remained silent. A funny feeling crept into my stomach.

"And now we're ready to write our paper?"

"Is the paper supposed to be about Megan Rinehart or her books?" asked Pete.

"Hmm. I'm not sure," I said.

"You aren't?" replied Logan. He looked worried.

"No. Are you? I mean, this is an author study project, but we've been researching our author's books, not her life."

"Maybe," Pete said slowly, "we could find out about Megan Rinehart's life and then see if it relates to what she writes about."

"That's a great idea!" I said.

"Brilliant," added Cokie. She yawned.

"So who's going to do what?" I asked. "Now we have to research Megan Rinehart and see how her life and her books relate. We could each write about one of the four books. And I'll be glad to start the research on Megan Rinehart," I offered.

"I'll be gl — "

"Logan?" Cokie didn't let him finish his sentence. "Are we going to the away game tonight? The one against Brick Township?"

I didn't know what Cokie was talking about — what sport, or even where Brick Township was. I just waited for Logan's answer.

"Sure," he replied.

Sure!? On a school night? With all this work to do? Where was Logan's brain? He must have left it at school. . . . Oh, wait. Forgive me. How could I have been so silly? Cokie had hypnotized Logan.

"I have an idea," spoke up Pete. (I never thought I'd be thinking this, but I sure was glad to have Pete Black on my side. First, he was honest enough to admit that he liked Megan Rinehart's books after all. Second, he was obviously involved in our project and was willing to work. Unlike some people I could think of.) "Why don't we *all* research Megan Rinehart now?" Pete suggested. "That seems fair."

"Sounds good to me, too," I replied, smiling at Pete.

"I have a question," said Cokie. "The four of us only have to hand in one project, right? Only one report is due?"

"Right," answered Logan.

"Just checking."

I changed my mind. Cokie wasn't just any old snake. She was a viper. I knew what she was getting at. She thought she could escape working on the project simply by leaving it up to the rest of us. She knew that *we* wanted a good grade.

"Well, the project is due in two weeks," I pointed out. "That isn't much time. Let's each choose one book to examine and then begin researching Megan Rinehart."

Which was exactly what we did.

A few minutes later, the meeting broke up. Cokie slid her arm around Logan's waist and they left Pete's house, heading, I guess, for Brick Township.

I felt disgusted. Not only was Logan wasting his time with Cokie, but I could see that Pete and I were going to end up doing the entire project ourselves.

CHAPTER 11

Our author projects were due on a Friday. By the Wednesday before, I was exhausted. So was Pete. I don't think I'd ever worked on an assignment so hard in my entire school career. For one thing, just as I'd feared, Pete and I did end up doing the project ourselves. For another, the kind of literary analysis we were doing (I just loved thinking of myself as a literary analyst or critic) was *hard*. In English class, we had analyzed poems and short stories and novels. But we had never done that in relationship to the author's *life*. Still, the work was interesting.

Pete and I could have killed Cokie and Logan, though. (Well, not really. But you know what I mean.) After the group meeting at Pete's house, he and I got right down to researching Megan Rinehart. We found more material than we'd expected. First we found two different books on authors and illustrators at the public library. Then, in our school library, we found a collection of pamphlets, each about an author or illustrator. Finally, Pete had the idea of checking both libraries to find out whether there were any articles about Megan Rinehart in periodicals or on microfilm. There were. In fact, there were six articles. So, armed with all that information, each of us (supposedly) began applying it to the book we'd chosen. (I had chosen the serious book, Pete had chosen the humorous one, Logan had said he'd take care of the mystery, and Cokie took the short-story collection, thinking it might be short. I was pretty sure she had not read it.)

When Pete and I had finished our researching and had written rough copies of our sections of the Megan Rinehart paper, we called another meeting.

Logan had not yet finished the research.

Cokie had not yet begun the research.

"What are we going to do?" I asked Pete, after Logan and Cokie had left the meeting early to buy new CDs or something.

"I guess we'll have to do Cokie and Logan's work for them. They keep promising they'll finish their sections on time, but do you believe them?"

"I certainly don't believe Cokie," I replied. "I don't know what to think about Logan. At least he's read the books — or most of them."

"We can't hand in a half-finished paper," said Pete.

"I know. Well, listen. You read all the books, right?" (Pete nodded.) "And so did I. I guess we'll just have to work on the mystery book and the short-story book, and finish the project ourselves. It isn't fair. But I don't want to blow my English average, especially over Megan Rinehart."

"All right." Pete paused thoughtfully. Then he went on, "But you know what? If you and I are going to do the whole project ourselves, then I think we should stop meeting with Cokie and Logan. They don't deserve to know what's going on."

"We-ell . . ." I kept thinking Logan would come around. He'd always been so responsible. Could Cokie really change him?

"I know Logan used to be your boyfriend," said Pete. "But come on. Give it a rest. He isn't being fair to us."

"Yeah. . . . Okay. From here on in, it's you and me."

That was before Mr. Kingbridge, our assistant principal, dropped his bombshell. Here's how unprepared I was for his announcement: If he had dropped a *real* bombshell, I wouldn't have been any more shocked.

It happened just two days before our author projects were due. In homeroom that morning, an announcement blared over the speaker system.

"All eighth-graders," said our school secretary, "are to report to the auditorium during third period. Mr. Kingbridge will be speaking to you. The subject of the assembly is the author projects. Attendance is required."

Well, that bit of news made me uneasy. But I still did not expect the bombshell that eventually dropped.

Third period.

I ran into Kristy and Dawn as we made our way into the auditorium.

"What do you think Kingbridge is going to say?" asked Kristy.

Dawn and I shook our heads. We couldn't imagine.

"Hey!" exclaimed Kristy as she found three seats together and quickly claimed them. "Maybe our teachers are giving us extra time to work on our projects. Or maybe they aren't due at all! Maybe Kingbridge decided our assignment was too taxing for thirteen-year-olds."

"Dream on," Dawn replied.

"Yeah," I said. "Anyway, after all the work

Pete and I have done, I *want* to hand in this paper. We deserve credit for it."

Kristy rolled her eyes.

I ignored her. My palms were sweating. What was Mr. Kingbridge going to say?

I did not have to wait long to find out. Five minutes later, he stepped up to the microphone that was standing in the center of the stage.

"I'm pleased to be the bearer of wonderful news," he began, "which I hope will both please and surprise each of you."

"Gag, gag," whispered Kristy.

"While you students have been researching authors and their books," Mr. Kingbridge continued, "the staff of the English department has been busy contacting many of the authors. And on Friday, when your projects are due, three of the authors will be here at Stoneybrook Middle School in *person*. Therefore, I declare Friday to be Author Day. And I am happy to announce that the authors who have agreed to travel to our school have also agreed to attend a special assembly at which the students who studied the authors will be granted the honor of presenting their projects orally, to the entire eighth grade and to the writers themselves. The three writers who will be present on Author Day are . . . Roger L. Willis,

T. J. Langston, and Megan Rinehart."

Kristy and Dawn both turned to me, their eyes bugging out.

"Megan Rinehart is coming *here?*" squeaked Dawn.

"I wonder if we'll get to shake her hand," said Kristy in an awed voice.

But all I could whisper was, "I have to give a talk on Megan Rinehart *to* Megan Rinehart? And to the whole eighth grade? And probably to all our teachers?"

"I bet the newspapers will cover the story," said Kristy.

Dawn elbowed her. "Time to close your mouth," she said. "Are you crazy? Mentioning reporters to Mary Anne? She's nervous enough about having to stand up and talk to everyone."

"I'll die," was all I could say. "I'll *die.*"

By the time school was over for the day, I had recovered slightly. I was still terrified of getting up in front of the eighth grade, and I was even more terrified that I'd say something about Megan Rinehart that she wouldn't like. But I'd had the presence of mind to find Pete and to call a group meeting for that very afternoon. I knew there was no way out of presenting our project — not with Megan Rinehart coming all the way from New York City and an assembly planned. So I would just have to stand on that stage in front of those hundreds of faces and talk. Even though it would be my personal version of a living nightmare.

The meeting was held at Pete's house, and he took charge. I knew he was incredibly excited about the idea of meeting a famous person.

"What we should do," he said importantly, "is each read the section of the project that we wrote." (I should mention that, as of that moment, neither Cokie nor Logan had given a section to Pete or me.)

"That sounds fair," I said.

Cokie and Logan blanched. They had been awfully quiet.

"Are you guys ready?" Pete asked them.

"Almost," said Logan.

"Well . . ." Cokie didn't finish her sentence.

"Great," said Pete quickly. "Just be ready by Friday. I guess that's it, you guys. Meeting adjourned." (He sounded like Kristy at a BSC meeting, but I didn't tell him so. I didn't think he'd appreciate it.)

What I did say was, "Pete, what are we going to do on Friday? You *know* Cokie hasn't finished her part of the project. And I can't tell whether Logan has. I don't want to present

Cokie's section for her. I'm just barely going to be able to get through my own. I *hate* talking in front of people."

Pete grinned. "No problem. You and I will hand in the complete written report and get a good grade. But at the assembly, you present your section, I'll present mine, and then Mr. Kingbridge and everyone will wait for Logan and Cokie to make their presentations. Our teachers will be able to tell right away who did the work and who didn't."

"*Oh,*" I said. I grinned, too. I was picturing Cokie on the stage in front of Mr. Kingbridge, our teachers, her friends, and Megan Rinehart. Everyone was waiting for her to speak. And she had nothing to say.

Then I pictured Logan in the same situation. My smile faded. Even after all we'd been through — the bad times, the arguments, Cokie — I didn't want to see him hurt or embarrassed. I wouldn't be able to stand that.

I liked Logan too much. (Didn't I?)

CHAPTER 12

"Oh, Tiggy, Tiggy, Tiggy."

I was lying on my bed and Tigger was with me. He was curled into the crook of my arm, purring loudly. He seemed to be purring *too* loudly for his small size. I bet his rumble could be heard downstairs.

I wished I were as happy as Tigger. *He* was the picture of contentment, his paws working in and out of the sleeve of my sweater (so what if he made a hole?), his eyes half closed, and the purring that made his little body tremble. *I* was a wreck.

The only things I could think about were Logan and Author Day.

And my thoughts were horribly confused. On the one hand, I missed Logan. I mean, I missed the relationship we used to have. On the other hand, I was angry at him for going out with Cokie. (I was also angry at me for allowing myself to feel hurt by that situation.)

On the *other* hand, I felt sorry for Logan, sorry for what might happen to him on Author Day. As I said before, I didn't want to see him embarrassed. But how was it possible to care about someone with whom I was so angry?

(Okay, I've just realized that I said I have three hands — on one hand, on the other hand, on the *other* hand. That may be an indication of how confused I felt.)

I looked at the clock in my bedroom. Almost four. In a little over an hour I would need to get ready for the day's meeting of the Baby-sitters Club. I hoped I would be able to pay attention at the meeting. Kristy hates when we don't pay attention. But my mind was on Logan. And Author Day.

In my head I was replaying, for about the zillionth time, the announcement Mr. Kingbridge had made earlier that day — when the phone rang.

"I'll get it!" I called, before remembering I was the only one home.

I ran into Dad and Sharon's room and picked up the extension. "Hello?"

"Hello . . . Mary Anne?"

"Yes?"

"This is Logan."

Was it possible that I'd forgotten the sound of his voice over the telephone? Or had I simply given up hoping to hear it again?

"Logan!" I said. "Um, hello."

"Hi. I was wondering. I mean . . . Look, I don't really know how to ask you this, but . . . All right. The thing is I think we need to work together."

"To get ready for Author Day?"

"Yeah."

Well. I couldn't believe this. Logan had frittered away his time with Cokie and now he was coming to *me* for help? (And I, who had just been feeling sorry for Logan, was now offended by his behavior, which seemed quite irresponsible? Nothing made sense anymore. Nothing.)

"Logan. I am not going to do your part of the project for you."

"You don't have to. It's written. But — "

"You mean you did the reading and the research?"

"Sure. The project's due in two days. I *better* have done the work."

"Oh."

"What aren't you saying, Mary Anne?" Logan asked. (That's how well we know each other.)

I had to tell Logan the truth. "I wasn't saying that — that I thought you hadn't done the project because you've been so busy with Cokie," I admitted.

I could hear Logan sigh. Then he said,

"Well, I *have* been busy with Cokie, but I still got my work done. Just barely." He paused. "She didn't, though."

"I didn't think so." Logan kept quiet. Finally I continued speaking. "If you've finished your section, then what do you need help with?"

"Don't you think I should know what you and Pete have been doing?"

"You know what we worked on."

"Yes, but shouldn't we rehearse together or plan together or something? You and Pete have been working by yourselves — "

"Because you and Cokie have been busy attending every movie ever made, and every single game at school."

"Mary Anne, let's not fight. We're supposed to be working as a group — and before you say anything, I *know* Cokie hasn't done her fair share, but let's forget about that, okay?"

"Okay."

"I want us to look good on Author Day. I especially want us to look good in front of Megan Rinehart. So can't we please get together?"

"You and Pete and I?"

"Or even just you and I. All I need is to see what's been written up so far. I have to make sure I'm on the right track."

Logan was asking for . . . well, not for help, exactly. But just to work with me. To coordinate with me. Of course I said yes.

"Great," replied Logan. "Thanks. When can I come over?"

"Let's see. I have a BSC meeting in a little while. But I don't have much homework tonight. You could come over after dinner. And after school tomorrow, if you want to."

"Terrific. Can I come at about seven tonight?"

"Sure."

"Okay. I'll see you then."

"See you."

I replaced the telephone receiver in its cradle.

Then I stood up and realized I was shaking.

In just a few short hours Logan and I would be together again. Alone.

"You mean you and Pete wrote up my section for me?" Logan was asking.

I nodded, my face reddening. "Cokie's, too," I added.

Logan and I had been together for barely five minutes. Were we going to fight again? I hoped not.

I knew I owed Logan an explanation, but I didn't want my entire family to hear it. So before I began to speak, I closed off the dining room, where we had spread out our books and papers.

"Pete and I felt we *had* to write up your sections," I told Logan quietly. "You guys didn't seem to be doing any work. And Cokie implied that she *wasn't* going to do any work. We didn't want to hand in an incomplete project, so we finished it ourselves, just to be on the safe side."

Logan lowered his eyes. "I guess I wasn't very responsible," he said. "I sort of let myself get swept away by Cokie — "

"Why?"

"Well, it sounds funny, but I missed having you around."

"You missed having *me* around, or you missed having a *girlfriend* around?"

"You! I missed you!" said Logan, exasperated. "But I didn't know what to do about it. And then there was Cokie. Obviously, she liked me. And she always wanted to go out and do things."

"Unlike me," I couldn't help adding.

"Unlike you," Logan agreed, to my surprise. "But we overdid it. We were *always* busy with something. My grades began to slip. And I just barely finished my section of the project. I was going to give it to you or Pete tomorrow. Then Mr. Kingbridge told us about Author Day. I had to break a date with Cokie to meet with you." Logan said something else then. I couldn't quite hear him. It sounded like, "Not that it matters," but I wasn't sure. "Anyway, I understand why you and Pete thought I hadn't done the work," Logan went on. "I never had the time to talk to you about it. Or maybe I never took the time. I don't know."

Logan looked so sad that I softened. "Oh, well. I guess it doesn't really matter, does it? We'll work together now. And we'll get rid of the section of the project that Pete and I wrote for you and replace it with the section you wrote yourself. Look. Here are the other sections that Pete and I did. Why don't you read them so you know what we've done, and I'll read yours?"

Logan relaxed. His shoulders had been hunched up around his ears. Now he lowered them. He let out a breath. "Okay. Thanks, Mary Anne." He slid a sheaf of papers across the table to me as I slid another sheaf to him. In the middle of the table, his fingers brushed mine lightly.

I had forgotten how soft his touch could be. No. That's not true. I had missed it so badly that I had *let* myself forget it. I wondered when Logan's hand would rest on mine again.

Logan and I worked until almost ten o'clock that night. He was right. We did need to coordinate what we were going to say. For one thing, he had found out some things about

Megan Rinehart that contradicted things Pete and I had discovered. So we called Pete, discussed our sources, and tried to get our facts straight. For another thing, Pete and I, working together, had organized our sections in the same way. Logan couldn't have known that. So in order for his section to fit in better with ours, he had to rearrange the way in which he was going to present his material. That took nearly three hours. By that time, it was Thursday afternoon. Pete and Logan and I had spent our lunch period together, and now Logan was at my house again. We were getting tired. But each time one of us would yawn, the other would say, "Just remember. We are going to *meet Megan Rinehart* tomorrow. It's worth all this work."

When Logan left my house, just before dinner, we thought we were prepared. We even thought our project was good. Maybe very good.

"I just hope Megan Rinehart likes it," I said.

"Quit worrying," was Logan's reply.

We laughed. He *always* used to tell me to quit worrying about one thing or another.

As he was leaving I called after him, "Keep your fingers crossed for tomorrow."

Logan held up crossed fingers. Then he climbed on his bicycle and rode off.

I turned around, closed the door, and leaned

against it. Phew. Logan was going to be okay when we gave our presentation.

But what about Cokie? Did she know what Logan was doing? Did she know she'd be the only unprepared group member on Author Day? Did she care? Did she assume that Logan would cover up for her? *Would* he cover up for her? I had no answers to my questions. But I guessed I would by this time the next day. The next day . . .

My heart beat wildly in my chest. The next day I would get to *meet Megan Rinehart.* I would also have to stand up in front of a million people and . . .

It was too scary to think about.

CHAPTER 13

Thursday

Ho-hum. I think I solved the Toilet Monster problem. My first time sitting for the Kormans since some person who shall remain nameless created a monster, and I solved the problem. It just took some creative thinking and a lot of talking. Also, you really have to understand children, which I do. I used to think of becoming a teacher, but now I'm changing my mind. Maybe I'll become a child psychologist instead.

Okay, okay. I know I'm way off the subject and also that I'm bragging. So here's what happened with Melody and Bill tonight....

While I was agonizing over the specter of Author Day, Kristy was agonizing over the specter of the Toilet Monster. Well, actually Bill and Melody were doing the agonizing. Kristy was trying to calm them down.

Mr. and Mrs. Korman left their house shortly after six-thirty on Thursday evening. Melody, Bill, and Skylar were finishing their supper. (Even though Kristy hadn't cooked it, the supper was hot dogs.)

Melody ate her last bite of hot dog with a flourish. "Yummy in my tummy," she said, wiping up a blob of ketchup with her finger.

"Towabumpa!" cried Skylar for no particular reason, except maybe that she was happy. She grinned at Kristy. (Skylar has, like, eight teeth.)

"Well, tonight's the night," said Bill ominously.

"What happens tonight?" Kristy wanted to know.

"Tonight . . . The Toilet Monster . . . will . . . appear," replied Bill in an eerie voice. He glanced at Melody.

"Oh! I forgot!" she exclaimed.

"We better go on a major monster hunt," added Bill.

"You guys, you do know that there isn't

really a Toilet Monster, don't you?" Kristy asked the older Korman kids.

"If there's no monster, then what growls?" Melody wanted to know.

"I . . . I'm not sure. Maybe there's a problem with your toilet tank."

"There's a big problem with it," agreed Bill. "The Toilet Monster lives there."

Skylar began banging on the tray of her high chair, a sign that she'd grown bored with eating. Kristy lifted her up, sat her by the sink (supporting her, of course), and began to wipe her off. Cleaning Skylar after a meal is sometimes quite a job since she usually eats with her hands — and then puts her hands on her face, or pats her head, or retrieves something from her lap. Presto! Food on her cheeks, in her hair, smeared onto her clothing. That's all part of being eighteen months old, I suppose.

Kristy concentrated so hard on cleaning Skylar that she didn't notice when Bill and Melody left the room. She set Skylar on the floor, turned around, and saw that the rest of the kitchen was empty.

"I wonder where your brother and sister went," said Kristy.

"Towabumpa," replied Skylar.

"Well, let's go see."

Kristy led Skylar into the front hall, then

carried her to the second floor which, she noticed, seemed a little too quiet.

"Melody? Bill?" called Kristy. "Time to put on your pajamas."

"Do we have to?" came a plaintive cry from Melody's room.

"Eventually, yes."

Kristy stood in the doorway to see what Melody was doing. The room looked empty. "Melody? Where are you?"

"Here."

"Where?"

"Here."

"*Where?*"

"Behind my chair."

Kristy stepped into the room and peered behind the armchair. Melody was crouched on the floor, hugging her knees.

"What are you doing back there?" asked Kristy.

"Hiding from the Toilet Monster."

Kristy sighed. "And where's Bill? Do you know?"

"He's hiding, too. I think he's in his closet."

"Listen," began Kristy. "I'm going to put Skylar to bed. When I'm finished, I want you and Bill to come out of hiding. I want to talk to you."

And that is just what Kristy did. She

changed Skylar's diaper, slipped a fresh pair of pajamas on her, and sang her to sleep. (Skylar happens to be very fond of the song "Breaking Up Is Hard to Do.")

Then Kristy gathered Bill and Melody in the playroom. This was not easy, since in order to get there, they had to pass the bathroom.

Melody ran by it with her fingers crossed, shouting, "Keep away, Mr. Toilet Monster!" Then she added to Kristy, "It's a good idea to be polite to the Toilet Monster. That's why I called him 'mister.' "

Bill ran by the bathroom, his arms flung up protecting his head, shouting, "Toilet Monster, be gone with you!"

At last Kristy and the kids were settled (oh, all right, huddled) on the couch in the playroom. "Now," began Kristy, "I want to tell you something."

"We already know," said Bill, and he parroted, "There's no such thing as the Toilet Monster. . . . Right? Is that what you were going to say?"

"No. I was going to say that lots of people have fears. Especially about going to bed. I have a cousin who gets into bed, but then she's afraid to go to sleep."

"Why?" asked Bill.

"Because she thinks something is under her bed."

"Ooh," said Melody in a trembly voice. "What?"

"A red mitten that snores."

Melody and Bill burst into laughter. "A snoring mitten!" hooted Bill.

"Isn't that silly?" said Kristy. "And I have a friend who used to have to *leap* way into and out of bed. She wouldn't let her feet get anywhere near the floor under the bed. She was afraid that if she did, they would get nipped by . . . "

"What?" asked Melody, wide-eyed but still smiling.

"Mr. and Mrs. Fox."

"Foxes?!" shrieked Bill.

"Shhh. Yes. They lived under the bed. They were married, I think. And the purpose — the *whole purpose* — of their lives was to bite people's feet. Of course, nobody ever saw them, and nobody's feet ever got nipped. You know why?"

"Because the foxes were imaginary," replied Bill.

"Yeah, pretend," agreed Melody.

"Exactly," said Kristy. "And guess what my mom used to be afraid of at bedtime."

"What?" wondered Bill and Melody.

"The Fur Thing." (The children's eyes were great, big question marks.) "My mom wasn't even sure what it was; just a *thing* that was *furry*."

"How old was your mom?" asked Bill suspiciously.

"When she believed in the Fur Thing? Oh, thirty-five or so," Kristy answered. The kids stared at her. "I'm *joking!*" exclaimed Kristy. "I think she was seven."

"My age," said Melody. "What did she think the Fur Thing would do?"

"Run out from under the bed and scream at her."

Melody and Bill couldn't help themselves. They began to laugh again and laughed so hard they nearly became hysterical. When Melody had regained some control of herself, she slid off the couch, scooted under a small table, then scooted out again, got to her feet, and screamed, "Aughhh!" Then she said, "Guess what I am."

"The Fur Thing!" cried Bill. And he screamed, too.

"Okay, quiet down, you guys," said Kristy. "Skylar's asleep — I hope."

"But the *Fur* Thing!" exclaimed Melody, still laughing. "That's so funny."

"As funny as the Toilet Monster?" asked Kristy.

The laughter stopped. Bill and Melody returned to the couch. Uh-oh, thought Kristy. And this was going so well.

However, a few moments later when she said that it was time to get ready for bed, the kids walked obediently down the hallway. They passed the doorway to the bathroom without crossing their fingers, covering their heads, or yelling. Presently, Bill went into the bathroom and closed the door. Kristy heard water running, and then the bathroom door opened and Bill returned calmly to his room.

"Bill, did you flush the toilet?" called Melody.

Silence. Then, "No . . . I guess I forgot."

"Boys," huffed Melody, and went into the bathroom herself. Kristy thought she was going to flush the toilet for Bill, but several minutes later, her teeth brushed and her face washed, she headed for her room.

"Toilet," Kristy reminded her from the hallway.

Melody paused. Kristy expected an argument, but instead Melody flushed the toilet — and then raced to her room and leaped into bed.

"Is the toilet still flushing?" she called.

"Yes," replied Kristy.

"Good," said Melody. "Then I made it."

"Made what?" Kristy furrowed her brow.

Melody giggled nervously. "I escaped from the Toilet Monster." She peeked at Kristy from under her covers, then added, "Just kidding."

Now, I didn't say anything to Kristy, but it was this last scene that made me wonder if the Toilet Monster had been banished after all. I had strong doubts. But Kristy thought she'd rid the Korman kids of their toilet problem forever. Especially when both Bill and Melody fell asleep quickly and easily. And stayed that way.

"We didn't have to go on any monster hunts," Kristy told me over the phone that night. "Nobody asked me to check in a closet or under a bed, and Melody stayed in her room. I've just been upstairs to look in on the kids. They're all where they're supposed to be."

"Well . . . great," I said. "That's really terrific. I mean it." My mind was on Author Day, of course, but Kristy sounded so satisfied with herself that I made a special effort to seem enthusiastic.

"So," said Kristy, "the Kormans aren't going to be home for another hour, and I want to talk to you about Author Day." (She did?) "But I better not stay on too long. You know."

I knew. The members of the BSC make a point of not carrying on long phone conversations while we're sitting. For one thing, the

118

parents of the children we're watching might be trying to reach us — to give us an important message — and they should be able to get through. For another thing, if the parents call home and keep getting a busy signal, they'll think they've hired a sitter who spends her time gabbing on the phone instead of being in charge of the kids. (In other words, instead of being responsible.)

"What about Author Day?" I asked Kristy.

"I just wondered how you were doing."

"I'm nervous."

"I'm not surprised."

We laughed.

"But I'm as ready as I can be."

"Good. . . . And Pete?"

"He's ready. And he'll love tomorrow. He likes being on stage. This project must be a dream come true for him. He's not going to fool around, though. He wants to impress Megan Rinehart. So do I. So does Logan." I waited for Kristy to say something, but she didn't. "And Logan's prepared," I went on.

"Is Cokie?" asked Kristy.

"That's the big mystery. I mean, I know she hasn't done her part of the project, but nobody has any idea what she's going to do tomorrow."

"Not even Logan?"

I shrugged, which was silly since Kristy

couldn't see me. "Maybe he knows by now. Maybe he talked to her tonight," I replied.

"Mmm. Listen, try not to be *too* nervous. Get some sleep tonight, okay? You don't want bags under your eyes when you meet Megan Rinehart."

"All right, Mom," I teased.

" 'Night, Mary Anne."

" 'Night, Kristy."

CHAPTER 14

It was Author Day.

On the stage in the SMS auditorium sat Megan Rinehart, Roger L. Willis, and T. J. Langston. The authors. At the microphone in the center of the stage stood Mr. Kingbridge. He looked out at the audience, which consisted not only of students and teachers, but parents and newspaper reporters as well.

"Will Logan Bruno, Cokie Mason, Mary Anne Spier, and Pete Black please come forward?" he said. "They are the final group to make a presentation today, and will be telling us about Ms. Rinehart and her work."

Logan, Pete, Cokie, and I were sitting in the first row of seats. We stood and walked up the stairs to the stage. I tripped over the top step, regained my balance, then bumped into Cokie, who was in front of me. After that my dress fell off and everyone, including my father and Megan Rinehart, howled with laughter.

Of course, none of that actually happened. It was just the way I imagined Author Day as I lay in bed at four-thirty that morning. I had awakened a little after four and was unable to go back to sleep.

The night before, Dawn had said to me, "If you want to do well at something that frightens you, then you have to *visualize* yourself doing well."

I never understand when Dawn starts talking about things like visualizing or channeling energy. "What?" I said.

"Imagine yourself on Author Day. Picture the program as you'd like to see it happen. That will give you confidence and make things go your way."

Well, here's how crazy I was over Author Day. First, I told Dawn I didn't believe that visualizing would work. Then, at four-thirty in the morning, I lay in bed and visualized the most awful things that could *possibly* happen. Even in a nightmare I don't think I would have tripped, lost my dress, and been laughed at by my father. However, once the image was in my head, it was hard to lose. *Then* I began to wonder if the image would make the awful things happen.

But you don't believe in visualizing, I told myself.

By the time I arrived at school on Friday, I was sane again, although tired. And I was a nervous wreck. Both Dad and Sharon had, at the last moment, taken the morning off from work so that they could attend the assembly. Dad was bringing his camera. (I was grateful that we do not own a *video* camera. Even so, the flashes would be pretty embarrassing.)

However, a teensy part of me was also excited. Three major authors were coming to *my* school! And, boy, was everyone making a big deal out of the event. Draped across the entrance to SMS was a colorful banner that read: WELCOME TO SMS AUTHOR DAY! The hallways were decorated with dust jackets from the books of Megan Rinehart, Roger L. Willis, and T. J. Langston, posters of the authors, buttons, bookmarks, and more. The kids in the computer classes had made fancy printouts illustrating the book titles. And Mr. Kingbridge was wearing a three-piece suit.

"Break a leg," Jessi said to me, as my friends and I split up for homeroom on Friday morning.

"Oh, I *hope* I don't," I said, thinking about the silly visualizing.

The program was to begin at ten o'clock and last for two hours. First, Mr. Kingbridge would make some remarks about our author projects. Then the three chosen projects would be presented. Then each of the authors would speak for a few minutes. Then the people in the audience could ask the authors questions. And finally Mr. Kingbridge would present the authors with gifts and thank-you certificates.

Okay. This is what *really* happened on Author Day.

At ten o'clock, Pete, Logan, I, and a distressed-looking Cokie were gathered backstage by Mr. Lehrer.

Good, I thought. This is a good sign. We're not sitting in the front row of the auditorium like we were in my vision.

"Your group," Mr. Lehrer told me, "will be the first to present a project. The microphone will be yours to use. When you have finished, please sit in the empty chairs behind the authors and stay on stage until the program is over. Any questions?"

Yes, I thought. Where's the nearest bathroom? I'm going to throw up.

But I didn't, even though the butterflies in my stomach were flapping wildly. I snuck a peek at Logan and caught his eye. He smiled at me. Then I smiled at Pete, who was watching Cokie shred a Kleenex into pieces so small you could barely see them.

And then I heard the microphone click on. Mr. Kingbridge began to speak. Pete, Logan, Cokie, and I jumped a mile. Instinctively, Logan and I reached out and grabbed hands. I must have been in shock about what was coming up because I didn't even think, I am actually *holding Logan's* hand again. I just stood there, listening to Mr. Kingbridge say how honored we were to be able to welcome into our school three such distinguished authors as those sitting on the stage. (Or something like that. In some situations, Mr. Kingbridge becomes a bit wordy. Around royalty he would probably be reduced to speaking nonsense: "Whereas turnarounds our hallowed halls do seek for the greater imperious notions of sanctified nations. Blither, blither, blither.")

All right. I'll get to the important things. Mr. Kingbridge made his remarks, then called our group onto the stage. With shaking knees I walked out from behind the curtain. I had never stood on the SMS stage before. I mean, not with the student body, parents, and teachers filling every available seat.

Flashes went off. Parents clapped. A few kids cheered. Kristy let loose with one of her ear-piercing whistles. And Pete began to speak. He reviewed the book he'd read and then commented on Megan Rinehart's life and how it related to the book. As I said, Pete loves to be onstage. But he was not a ham. His talk was well organized, and Pete knew how to look at the audience while he spoke. He even looked over at Megan Rinehart a couple of times. When he finished, the audience applauded and Ms. Rinehart smiled.

I was next.

Pete nudged me gently toward the microphone. My voice shaking, I read my entire speech. I never once looked up from my paper. But when I finished, the audience applauded loudly for me. I guess they liked what I had to say, even if I didn't say it very well.

Then it was Logan's turn. As a speaker, he fell somewhere between Pete and me. Once, I glanced at Mr. Kingbridge while Logan was talking, and saw him nodding his head. The extra time that Logan and I worked together had paid off. I felt relieved . . . until Cokie stepped up to the mike.

The first thing she did was cast a bewildered, nervous glance at Logan and Pete and me, as if to ask, "How did you *do* that?" Then she looked down at the single sheet of notebook paper she was holding.

"Well," began Cokie, "I read this really good book by Megan Rinehart." Then Cokie gave a description of the contents of the short-story book. The description sounded familiar. After a few minutes, I recognized it as the summary that was written on the jacket flaps of the book. Cokie had copied it word for word.

Logan recognized it, too. He began to whisper along with Cokie: " . . . powerful, tautly told tales, peopled with an array of unique characters more often found in . . . "

I nearly giggled. Then I elbowed Logan. He stopped whispering. But for the next few moments neither he nor Pete nor I could look at one another.

Cokie finished cribbing from the book jacket, thanked Megan Rinehart for being her "very most favorite author in the world," and sat down next to Pete. She tried to look self-satisfied, but when she saw our faces — and when she heard the mere smattering of applause the audience was able to muster — she blushed, and the smile faded from her mouth.

The program continued.

My part was over and I sighed with relief. I even found the courage to look out at the audience while the next two groups presented their projects. After some searching I found Kristy and Dawn (sitting together), Mallory (surprisingly, *not* sitting anywhere near Jessi), Dad, and Sharon. And Grace Blume. I smiled at my friends and at Dad and Sharon. But I didn't let my gaze meet Grace's. I knew she would make a horrible face at me.

Twelve o'clock came around much faster than I'd thought it would. Had I really been sitting on a stage in front of hundreds of people for *two hours?* I felt unreal. But all the projects had been presented, the authors had spoken (Megan Rinehart was fascinating; I think she was the best speaker of all), and the audience members had asked their questions. After awhile the questioning got out of hand. Didn't anybody *listen* to anyone else? People asked the same questions over and over. For instance, someone asked Megan Rinehart where she got her story ideas, and then, like, two minutes later, Cokie asked her the same question. (The people onstage, even Mr. Kingbridge, were allowed to ask questions, too.) Anyway, everyone sort of tittered when Cokie repeated the question, but Ms. Rinehart was very patient and just repeated the answer she'd given before. Pete, however, elbowed Cokie and whispered loudly, "She just *an-*swered that question, jerk." Cokie blushed again and I *almost* felt sorry for her.

When the question-and-answer time was over, Mr. Kingbridge presented each author with an SMS T-shirt and mug, and a thank-you certificate. The program was over. The curtain closed.

Guess what happened then. Megan Rinehart stood up and walked right over to *me*. "Congratulations," she said. "That was a wonderful talk."

I tried to smile, but my mouth muscles just kind of twitched. "I — I'm not much of a speaker," I stammered. "But I do love your books. I've been reading them for several years. I think I've read everything you've written."

"What a nice compliment." Ms. Rinehart smiled at me. Then she spoke to Logan and Pete. She looked around for Cokie, but Cokie had nipped offstage the second the curtain had fallen. Because of that, Cokie missed getting a *signed* copy of Megan Rinehart's newest book. She'd brought one for each of us group members.

A signed copy. I would never, ever part with it.

I wished I could talk to Megan Rinehart forever, but she had to leave.

Logan and I walked off the stage together.

"We did it," said Logan.

"Yeah, it's over. And it wasn't so bad. *And* we got to meet a famous author."

"Mary Anne?" Logan sounded thoughtful. "Would you like to go out for dinner tomorrow night? I mean, if it's convenient for you. It'll be my way of saying thanks for your help."

I knew Logan and I had a lot more than "thank you" and "you're welcome" to say to each other. So of course I said I'd love to have dinner with him.

"Great," replied Logan with relief. "I'll call you tomorrow."

CHAPTER 15

I never once doubted that Logan would call me that next day. The old Mary Anne might have — the Mary Anne who was rarely able to stand up for herself, to say what she really wanted or really felt; who hadn't survived working in a group that included Logan and Cokie; who hadn't given a talk to hundreds of people and heard applause when she finished; who hadn't met a famous author and been complimented by her. The new Mary Anne — the one who had done all those things, and survived life without Logan — the new Mary Anne was confident that he would phone. And he did.

That's not to say that my heart didn't begin to pound when Dawn called to me and told me who was on the phone. My heart *raced*. I was so happy. I was going to see Logan again, that very night.

"Hi," he said. "What do you want to do this evening?"

"I thought you wanted to go out to dinner."

"I do, but only if that's really okay with you."

"It's really okay. Let's go someplace quiet."

"How about the new health food restaurant?"

"Logan, I live with *Dawn!*" I exclaimed.

Logan laughed. "All right. How about the Italian restaurant?"

"Perfect."

We agreed to meet there at seven o'clock.

"Won't it be great," I said to Dawn later, as she helped me choose an outfit to wear to dinner, "when we're old enough to drive? Then our parents won't have to chauffeur us everywhere. Just think — Logan will have, say, a red convertible, and he'll swing by and pick me up when we go out."

"Or maybe *you'll* have the red convertible," replied Dawn. "And *you'll* swing by the Brunos' house and pick up *Logan* for dates."

"Yeah." I stared dreamily into space. Then I fell out of orbit and returned to Earth. "What am I saying?" I exclaimed. "I'm talking like Logan and I are a couple again."

"A couple of what?" teased Dawn.

I didn't smile. "This is serious," I told my sister. "Logan hasn't said anything about getting back together. But I'm assuming it's going to happen."

"Are you ready to get back together with him?" Dawn asked. "Remember how trapped you felt before. You felt like Logan was running your life."

"But now I miss him. And anyway, I don't think I'm going to *let* Logan or anyone else run my life. I can do that for myself. . . . What do you think of this outfit?" I held up an oversized blue top and a pair of red tights.

"I think your father won't let you out of the house in it."

"Yes, he will. When I bought it, he said, 'Mary Anne, that's much too revealing,' and I said, 'It's not nearly as revealing as a bathing suit,' and he said, 'That's true,' so I got to keep it."

Dawn laughed. "Good luck tonight," she said.

"Thanks," I replied. But I didn't think I would need it. I would be able to handle things just fine on my own.

Logan and I arrived at the restaurant at the same time, so we were able to walk inside together. In fact, as soon as we *were* inside, Logan slipped his arm through mine. Was he just being polite? Or did that mean something more?

I decided not to overanalyze everything.

A waiter showed us to an empty table. When he left, Logan and I slipped off our jackets.

"Great outfit!" exclaimed Logan.

"Thanks," I replied. And then, before he could say anything, I added, "Dad approved."

"How did you know I was going to ask?"

"Because I'm Mary Anne and you're Logan."

"Right."

We ordered Cokes and then opened the menus. As soon as the waiter had written everything down and had left carrying the menus, Logan said simply, "We have to talk."

"I know."

"Do you want to go first?"

I hesitated. Then I said, "All right," and drew in a shaky breath. "I miss you."

"I miss you, too." Logan reached across the table and took one of my hands. He held it, rubbing it gently as I continued to speak.

"I hardly even remember why we stopped talking to each other."

"Neither do I."

"But what about Cokie?"

Logan looked as if I'd just said, "So who's your pick for the World Series?"

"Huh?" was his answer. "Cokie?"

"Yeah, you remember. The person you've been dating for the last month or so."

"She doesn't mean anything to me."

"Nothing?"

"Well, hardly anything. She's fun, Mary Anne. But she isn't you."

"Is that good or bad?" I dared to ask.

I thought Logan might get exasperated. Instead, he frowned, concentrating. "It's good," he said finally. "I mean, I guess it's good. This hasn't been an easy month for me, you know. Since I let Cokie talk me into going out with her so much, my grades dropped. I almost messed up on the author project, and — and I hurt Cokie, which I really didn't mean to do. I don't like hurting anybody. Besides, Cokie didn't plan to mess me up. And in the end, *she* was the one who got messed up."

I thought about that. It made sense. Cokie flaunted her relationship with Logan. She also truly liked him. She hadn't set out to make my life miserable. She just had a crush on Logan. That was something I could certainly understand.

"What did Cokie say about Author Day?" I asked Logan.

"I don't know. I haven't spoken to her. She must realize that the foul-up was her fault. She also must be pretty mad at me. She'll just have to get over that, though."

"Do you think you'll see her again?"

"Only in school. No more dates. That's over."

Our food arrived then, and I decided we should talk about something a little lighter. The food was heavy enough. I didn't want to add a heavy conversation to it. So I told Logan about the Toilet Monster.

He laughed. Then he said, "And now the monster is gone for good?"

"That's what Kristy thought," I replied. "But she was wrong. The next time she sat at the Kormans', Melody and Bill still had to race into their beds while the toilet was flushing."

"Maybe you could invent games about the monster," suggested Logan. "That would make him seem fun instead of scary."

"What kind of games?" I asked.

"Um, let's see. Like timing the kids when they run to their beds and seeing who's faster. Or asking them to draw pictures of the Toilet Monster. Then point out the silly or funny things in the pictures. Or make up stories about the monster. I bet that pretty soon he'll just be part of the kids' imagination."

"Logan, that's a great idea!" I exclaimed. "I'll mention it at the next BSC meeting."

When the waiter had cleared away our dinner dishes and brought Logan and me a huge ice-cream sundae to share, Logan grew very quiet.

"What's wrong?" I asked.

Logan fiddled around with his spoon. "Our dinner's almost over and I haven't said what I really wanted to say tonight."

"You mean, 'Thank you'?"

" 'Thank you?' "

"Mm-hmm. Yesterday you said you wanted to take me to dinner as a way of thanking me for giving you a hand with the project."

"Oh. Right."

"So you're welcome."

"But it isn't that, Mary Anne. That's not the real reason."

"It isn't?" I whispered, and my poor old heart began to pound again.

"No. I want to ask you something."

"Okay."

"Do you want to go out again sometime?"

"You mean on a real date?"

Logan relaxed a little. He smiled. "Yes, on a real date. I still care about you, Mary Anne. I care a lot."

"Me, too. And I've *really* missed you."

"Same here."

We decided we'd try getting together on Friday night. But I knew we'd see a lot of each other before then. I was pretty sure Logan would begin eating lunch with my friends and me again. And he'd hang around my locker before and after school and between classes, too.

And we would talk on the phone at night, just like in the old days.

Since I knew all this, I wasn't too surprised when our phone rang not long after I got home that night. I dashed into the kitchen, picked up the extension, and said, "Hi, Logan."

"Hi." (He didn't need to ask how I had known he was the caller.) "So what are you doing tomorrow?"

"Dawn and Claud and I are going to the mall." I doodled on a piece of scrap paper.

In another lifetime, Logan would have said, "Cancel your plans and come to the movies with me," or something like that. But now he said, "Okay. Have fun. I'll see you in school on Monday, but maybe we'll talk before then."

"Maybe?" I repeated. "Definitely." Doodle, doodle.

"Great. I'll call tomorrow."

"Good night, Logan." I hung up the phone and looked at my scrap paper. In tiny letters, I had written: MAS + LB 4-Ever.

About the Author

ANN M. MARTIN did *a lot* of baby-sitting when she was growing up in Princeton, New Jersey. Now her favorite baby-sitting charge is her cat, Mouse, who lives with her in her Manhattan apartment.

Ann Martin's Apple Paperbacks include *Yours Turly, Shirley; Ten Kids, No Pets; With You and Without You; Bummer Summer;* and all the other books in the Baby-sitters Club series.

She is a former editor of books for children, and was graduated from Smith College. She likes ice cream, the beach, and *I Love Lucy;* and she hates to cook.

Look for #47

MALLORY ON STRIKE

Mary Anne checked the club notebook and shook her head. "Boy, we're really filled up on Saturday. We just booked four of us today, and Claudia and Stacey already have jobs. It looks like Mallory's the only one who can do it."

Kristy turned and smiled at me. "Lucky you. It sounds like you'll be able to earn a lot of money on this one."

I ran it over in my head quickly. If I sat for the Hobarts on Saturdays, that would only leave me one day each weekend to work on my story, finish my homework, and do chores for my family. That just wasn't enough time. It was a tough decision, but I had to make it.

"I'm sorry, Mary Anne," I said, "but I have to turn this one down."

Everyone stared at me in surprise. "Do you already have another sitting job?" Stacey asked.

I shook my head. "No. I just would rather not take this one, if that's okay."

I was about to tell the club about Young Authors Day, and how important the contest was to me, but the looks on their faces made me stop. I was afraid they'd think I was being stupid and selfish. I pursed my lips and stared at my hands in my lap, hoping they'd stop staring at me.

"Well . . ." Mary Anne shrugged. Her voice trailed off as she studied the notebook. "I think that means we'll have to call one of our associate members."

Kristy picked up the phone. "I'll call Shannon Kilbourne. She told me she needed some work."

I didn't look up for the rest of the meeting. I was too embarrassed. Luckily it lasted only a few more minutes. At six o'clock, when Kristy announced that the meeting of the BSC was officially adjourned, I hurried out of the Kishi house and grabbed my bike. I didn't even wait to talk to Jessi. My feelings were too jumbled up. I needed time to think.

**Read all the books
in the Baby-sitters Club series
by Ann M. Martin**

142

144

THE BABY-SITTERS CLUB®

by Ann M. Martin

More titles... ▶

The Baby-sitters Club titles continued...

Available wherever you buy books...or use this order form.

Scholastic Inc., P.O. Box 7502, 2931 E. McCarty Street, Jefferson City, MO 65102

Please send me the books I have checked above. I am enclosing $_____
(please add $2.00 to cover shipping and handling). Send check or money order - no
cash or C.O.D.s please.

Name _____

Address _____

City_____ State/Zip_____

Tell us your birth date! _____

BSC792

Don't miss out!

Join the

BABY SITTERS®

Fan Club!

Pssst... Know what? You can find out **everything** there is to know about *The Baby-sitters Club*. Join the BABY-SITTERS FAN CLUB! Get the hot news on the series, the inside scoop on all the Baby-sitters, and lots of baby-sitting fun...just for $4.95!

With your **two-year** membership, you get:

- ★ An official membership card!
- ★ A colorful banner!
- ★ The exclusive Baby-sitters Fan Club quarterly newsletter with baby-sitting tips, activities and more!

Just fill in the coupon below and mail with payment to:
THE BABY-SITTERS FAN CLUB,
Scholastic Inc., P.O. Box 7500, 2931 E. McCarty Street, Jefferson City, MO 65012.

- -

The Baby-sitters Fan Club

❑ **YES!** Enroll me in The Baby-sitters Fan Club! I've enclosed my check or money order (no cash please) for $4.95 made payable to Scholastic Inc.

Name _____ Age _____

Street _____

City _____ State/Zip _____

Where did you buy this *Baby-sitters Club* book?

| ❑ Bookstore | ❑ Drugstore | ❑ Supermarket | ❑ Book Club |
| ❑ Book Fair | ❑ Other_____(specify) | | |

Not available outside of U.S. and Canada.

BSC791